The Deliverance of Holly

By Taylor Painter

Published by Forget Me Not Romances, an imprint of Winged Publications

Copyright © 2025 by Taylor Painter

This is a work of fiction. All characters, names, dialogue, incidents, and places either are the product of the author's imagination or are used fictitiously. Any resemblance to actual events, locales, or people, living or dead, is entirely coincidental.

ISBN-13:978-1-968792-50-3

Prologue

As told in *The Primrose of Bascomb* and its sequel, *Violet's Roots,* a young Blaire had found a diary belonging to an eccentric midwife named Addie. Blaire came to know and love Addie through the words written in the lost diary, only to discover that she'd bought the very home Addie had lived in before passing away. Not only would Blaire be making her home in the very place where the words in the beloved diary were recorded, but she also discovered that Addie was a woman whom she'd cared for in *Sunny Meadows* nursing home, where Blaire worked as a nurse.

Two years after making these stunning discoveries, Blaire met a woman named Violet, with who she bonded and desired to form her life after. As the two women became closer, they began to realize that they had more in common than they'd originally believed. Violet revealed that she'd visited Blaire's house countless times as a child, as her mother, Madge, was

Addie's truest friend. The two young women became inseparable friends as they talked about the strong thread that bound them together: Addie.

But after exploring further into Addie's handwritten diaries found in the old farmhouse that she'd settled into, Blaire uncovered that Violet was much more than a friend…she was also the half-sister she never knew she had…

"Fulfillment"

ONE

It had been a long walk through the chilly, salty town, and Holly's feet ached. She longed for somewhere–anywhere– to prop them up and to lay her head down. The nice waitress who'd been taking a smoke break at Skippy's Shrimp Shack had offered her a paper basket of cold hushpuppies and a cup of syrupy-sweet tea, for which she was grateful. When prodded with nosy questions, Holly had lied and told the waitress that her name was Jessica and she was just out taking a walk in hopes of inducing her labor. She'd told her she was from the area – just a block down the homey beachfront street.

The truth was that Holly was from Tennessee, an eight-hour drive from the bustling streets of coastal South Carolina. Holly had landed here after having run out of bus ticket money a few towns back. Since then, she'd been walking. To where? She wasn't sure, but she knew she was going to have to find a place to hunker down soon.

The night air cut like a knife as Holly wrapped her coat tightly around her large, round belly and glanced over her shoulder for the thousandth time. Surely he wouldn't find her here. Nobody would ever suspect Holly to take off to a place like the coast, whether a week before Christmas or the middle of Summer. The ocean had never appealed much to Holly. She belonged on the snowcapped mountain, in Grandpa's cabin, where she'd breathed nearly every breath of her life for as long as she could remember. She longed to be sitting next to Grandpa by the crackling fire, listening to the staticky radio on the windowsill.

Her heart would always be there, no matter how far she had to run to hide from Colt. The last thing he'd said to her before he released his tight grip from her long, blonde hair was, "Try'n run from me, 'n you'll end up dead, just like ye Grandpaw."

Of course, he was drunk when he'd said it, like he was more than half the time. But Holly knew he was mean enough to kill her if he set his mind to it, whether he was drunk or not. After he'd swerved backward all over the long dirt driveway in his beat-up, dirty old pickup truck, Holly quickly packed a backpack full of necessities and emptied the savings jar Grandpa had kept in the kitchen cupboard. Without Grandpa there, Holly knew she would have to protect herself and the baby one way or the other. Once Colt was out of sight, and the night was quiet, she scurried to the small bus station in the dark, catching the first Greyhound she could catch.

Ever since the bus let her off in Charleston, she'd meandered around town, scoping out the businesses - anywhere she could sneak into before closing time and hide out, hoping nobody would see her before they'd locked the doors and left for the night. She spent three nights at Sandy's Seafood Buffet, sleeping on a cushioned vinyl booth, using her blue cardigan that smelled like home as a blanket. It was lonely, but safe. He wouldn't find her there.

Holly woke in the early morning hours and crept into the large kitchen where she raided the leftovers that had been stored in the fridge. Each morning, she took just enough Captain's Wafer crackers and containers of whipped butter to keep her from starving, drank a glass of water, and spent the day wandering aimlessly around town, trying not to be noticed. There, she studied businesses and homes, learning the behaviors of the business owners. Were any of them caring enough to conceal her if she could work up the nerve to ask someone? Would they turn her in to the police right away for loitering and trespassing? If Colt *did* track her this far, would any of them see past his 'good ole boy' facade and tell him they'd seen a blonde-haired pregnant girl around here?

Even after sneakily observing and listening to private conversations from the dark shadows the restaurant and store buildings cast against the street lamps above, Holly wasn't sure of anything other than the fact that she could trust no one. The only person she could trust was gone. Her heart ached at the thought of Grandpa.

She could see him each time she closed her eyes, sitting at the dining table wearing denim overalls over his robust midsection and sipping coffee from a saucer. He hadn't been mad at her for running off with Colt in the middle of the night, even though she knew better. She learned too late what a mistake that had been.

Once she decided to move on from Sandy's seafood joint, she came upon another hole-in-the-wall restaurant, further into town and closer to the beach. She knew time was running out. For one thing, it was surely getting close to the time for the baby to be born. She figured most places would close down for at least a few days for Christmas.

Holly had hoped she could find a place with the soft booths or, at the very least, carpet in the dining room in which she'd sleep on, using her backpack as a pillow. The longer the place was closed down for Christmas, the better. She would be just fine holed up in one of those restaurants until they reopened. She could prepare food for herself in the kitchen, have running water and towels to bathe with, a toilet, and most importantly–safe shelter. She would manage nicely for several days. Maybe she'd even get a full week in one place without having to show her face in the public eye, but she'd have to find the right one. This town wasn't a tourist attraction. It was a small, bustling town where residents supported the local businesses year-round.

As she walked the sidewalk, the chilly afternoon air sent shivers up and down her spine. She looked down at her round belly as she walked, looking up only to see the hours posted on the signs in front of the glowing restaurant windows. She knew she had to keep moving. If she stayed in one part of this town for too long, people would begin to talk. Curiosity would surely get the best of them if anyone noticed her idleness. Holly imagined the small coastal community to be one where people noticed outsiders and then rushed to call their neighbors about them.

She decided she would tell anyone who asked that her name was Amanda. She was just walking around as much as possible to try to jumpstart her labor, she'd say. She only lived a mile down the street in one of those apartments with the palm trees out front. All of those things were the opposite of the truth, of course. Though Holly was currently a squatter from out of town, those ritzy apartments were a far cry from her log cabin in the country. And jumpstarting her labor was the last thing she wanted to do. She pushed the thought from her mind and briefly concerned herself with the livestock back at home. They could drink from the pond – it wouldn't be frozen, but no one was there to feed them their hay. There was nothing she could do about it, though. More pressing matters took precedence then, and even now, as Holly carefully searched for a place to take shelter. Christmas was coming, but it meant nothing to her as she sought to survive for the sake of her unborn baby.

As Holly neared the end of the street, the businesses became fewer. She continued to saunter a short distance until she laid her eyes on a small, yellow cottage that attracted her from afar. There was no car in the driveway. It was the only house on the street without the glow of Christmas lights. But the evergreen shrubs out front were neatly trimmed, and the clean, white picket fence along the walkway was straight and intact. There was no mailbox, Holly noticed. A vacation home, perhaps?

Pacing slowly up the walkway toward the house, Holly casually glanced around at her surroundings. The street was quiet and peaceful, and there was no one outside at any of the neighboring houses.

She climbed the steep steps up onto the painted gray porch and approached the front door. Rapping on the solid wooden door several times, Holly dropped her hand and listened closely for a stir inside the quaint cottage.

Ten seconds pass. Fifteen. No signs of anyone home. It was completely dark inside. Again, she gave a hearty knock on the maroon-painted door, a little harder the second time. She waited, nervously planning to ask to use the restroom if anyone ever opened the door. Nobody would deny a pregnant woman the use of their restroom, would they?

After standing on the doormat listening through the door for nearly a minute, Holly decided to give the knob a gentle try. Just in case of the off-chance it was unlocked. If she discovered anyone inside, she'd apologize profusely for entering the wrong home. "I must be on the wrong street…I'm visiting my aunt for Christmas, and this house looks just like how I remember hers…I think the end of pregnancy jitters are starting to get to me…" she'd sputter. Surely that would suffice, she thought.

Slowly, quietly, Holly twisted the cold brass doorknob to the left. It turned. She gave the door a gentle push, and surprisingly, it opened right up, startling her a bit. Thinking quickly, she called out from the door, "Matthew! I'm b-a-a-a-c-k! Are you here?"

Not a sound was heard in return. Holly opened the door a bit wider and stuck her head in through the crack she'd made.

"Matthew?" she called, a bit louder. No answer.

Finally, after scanning the street for any dangers of being seen by anyone, Holly stepped inside the quiet home and quickly shut the door behind her. She felt along the wall until she found the light switch, and then she carefully scanned her surroundings. Hanging on the wall to the left of Holly were four interesting pieces of artwork. Each in slightly different sized frames, there were names spelled out in seashells against a cream-colored piece of linen and placed in a vertical row down the sand-colored wall.

First, there was *Madge*. Below that, *Addie*. Next, *Violet*. And then *Blaire*.

Holly studied the names for a moment, wondering who they might be. Sisters, perhaps?

She locked the door behind her before dropping the weight of her backpack on the hardwood floor. After slipping her shoes off her tired, swollen feet, she slowly began to explore the vacant home. The fears of getting caught inside faded a bit as she grew excited about the discovery of the warm house.

Holly knew the comfort she felt within the walls of the cottage couldn't be threatened by the thought of someone finding her there. If it happened, she'd manage. But she was behind closed doors in an actual house now, two states away in the unlikeliest of places. She felt the weight of what felt like the whole world fall from her shoulders and melt onto the floor beneath her aching feet. She wouldn't step foot back outside the cottage until she had to. Nobody else would catch a glimpse of her in this town, just like nobody had seen her enter the unlocked beach house.

The place was decorated simply but beautifully. There was wicker furniture with fluffy pastel cushions and glass bowls full of shells sitting on just about every surface in the small living room. There were genuine oil paintings hanging on the walls, displaying beautiful strokes that had created images of wildlife and enchanting scenes. There were beeswax pillar candles perched nicely in handmade pottery holders. There was a record player with a shiny black record sitting on its idle platter. Holly padded around the room, taking in each artifact and treasure that seemed to be permanently ingrained in the home, though without a speck of dust to be seen.

She noticed that there was no television, and it was just as well because she wouldn't risk any passersby taking notice of someone staying in the house anyway. At night, she supposed, she'd keep the lights off. She was used to the dark by now.

The cozy, eclectic living room was joined to a small kitchen with a single, tiny dining table beside a plaid curtain-drawn window. Beside the vintage avocado-green stove was a primitive wooden hutch housing rows of glass jars. As Holly moved closer to the cabinet, she studied the contents of the beautifully displayed jars and found that they were each full of dry goods—beans, rice, pasta, popping corn, herbs.

Nearby, the soft hum of the refrigerator beckoned her toward it, adding a layer of excitement to the newly discovered dry goods. She would gladly prepare beans and rice for herself. It would surely beat what she'd been eating for the last week. As she stood in front of the bulky, green metal box that matched the stove, she held her breath in anticipation.

She cracked the door, the light inside the refrigerator flashing on. As she opened the door wider, she gasped aloud at the sight. The drawers and shelves appeared to be fully stocked, food stacked neatly on each one. Holly reached for the full bottle of grapefruit juice first. Checking the date, she was relieved that it didn't expire for another two weeks. Placing the bottle back on the shelf, she grabbed a container of yogurt and inspected it as well.

"Hmm. It's still good," she said aloud with wonder.

There were apples, oranges, grapes, cheeses, a tightly wrapped loaf of what appeared to be homemade bread, pickles, and eggs. Holly couldn't believe her eyes, though she was growing more convinced that this must be someone's home. They'd surely be back soon, she thought. But she was nearly in survival mode upon stumbling upon the place, so she fed herself a snack of fruit and cheese as quickly as possible before taking a few apples and oranges back to her bag by the door, just in case.

After stashing the fruit inside and zipping the backpack up, Holly flipped on a small table lamp in the corner of the living room and turned the overhead light off. Then, she peeked out the small, slim window on the front door. The street still looked vacant, though there was now a vehicle parked in the driveway across the street. Walking the short distance back through the small living room and into the kitchen, Holly decided to check out the only other rooms in the house – the bedroom and attached bathroom.

Through a doorway from the side of the kitchen,

Holly found the sleeping quarters. Adorned with a four-poster queen-sized bed and matching furniture, the room looked immensely inviting. The bedding was thick, plush, and the prettiest shade of peach. With soft pillows stacked against the headboard and a lamp by the bed, Holly wanted so badly to lie down. She massaged her large, round belly before walking slowly around the corner and into the small restroom.

There was no toothbrush or toiletries displayed on the white pedestal sink, Holly noticed at once. She stepped onto the pastel blue rug in front of the sink; the plush foam material felt good on her bare feet.

She looked at her reflection in the oval mirror above the sink. "I look awful," she said to herself, rubbing her hands across her cheeks. Her greasy hair was slicked back into a bun; she couldn't remember the last time she'd shampooed it. Her face was pale with dark circles beneath her blue eyes.

Finally, she ran her hand along the back of the mirror and discovered that it was a cabinet. Opening it, Holly was pleasantly surprised to see that it was nearly empty, holding only a bottle of Aspirin and a pair of fingernail clippers. A sign in her favor that the cottage wasn't a full-time residence.

Closing the cabinet, Holly moved over to the shower and pulled the cloth curtain back. There was a bottle of shampoo and a bar of soap, barely used. The thought of a hot shower was thrilling to Holly. Turning from the shower, she carefully rummaged through the wooden cabinet above the toilet and selected an extra soft towel and washcloth. Quickly, she turned the water on nearly as hot as it would go before scurrying to retrieve her backpack from where she'd left it by the door.

As she picked the bag up from the floor, she peeked out the front window once more. Still, nobody was to be seen. Making sure the door was locked, Holly nearly skipped back through the bedroom and into the bathroom.

Hurriedly, she unpacked a clean T-shirt, jogging pants, socks, and underwear and laid them on top of the bag before undressing and stepping into the steamy shower. The warm water was most satisfying. She wanted to stay and enjoy it longer, but thought it best to wash herself and get out of the shower. Should someone happen to walk in, she'd prefer not to be in such a compromising situation. Not to mention, she couldn't hear if anyone approached over the sound of the shower.

Nevertheless, it was delightful and refreshing. Holly dressed herself and brushed her clean, wet hair with a brush she'd somehow thought to pack. She looked into the mirror again; she was relieved to see that getting clean improved her appearance significantly.

Holly toweled the ends of her long blonde hair once more before hanging the towel up to dry on a brass rod. Then, feeling rejuvenated, she padded softly through the bedroom, wearing her only pair of clean socks. She'd been relieved to discover a washing machine and dryer at the end of the short hallway just outside the bathroom. Maybe she'd get to use it, she thought.

But first, she headed for the kitchen where she sliced a thick piece of bread from the hunk in the refrigerator and popped it into the toaster. While she waited for the bread to toast, she found the butter to slather on top and poured herself a tall glass of milk.

The warm, buttered bread was most fulfilling. Holly thought of Grandpa, and a pang of sadness taunted her. Grandpa loved buttered toast and black coffee together. Holly thought she'd look for some coffee in the house tomorrow, if nobody showed up and ran her out. She was unsure how she'd repay the owners of the food she'd so luckily found, but she decided she could worry about that later.

After the toast and milk, she had a chilled Macintosh apple, eating every bite but the stem. Then, she went to the sink and washed the dirty milk glass before meandering to the bedroom.

The big bed was so soft and inviting. The clock on the wall read six-thirty. Holly made sure all the lights and lamps in the small house were turned off before she slowly climbed onto the big bed and pulled the thick plush blankets over her shoulders. As she lay still and quiet on her right side, she felt the thumps of the baby moving inside her. She placed her hands on her large belly, cradling it, and drifted off to sleep to the drumming of the baby's gentle kicks against her palms and the distant, rhythmic sound of crashing waves.

TWO

Holly awoke to the sound of seagulls squawking and sunlight leaking in around the blinds over the slim bedroom windows. The wall clock read eight o'clock. She'd slept for more than thirteen hours in the solace of the foreign bed.

Sitting up had become nearly impossible given the size of her belly, so Holly rolled off the side of the bed and briefly stretched as she stood, before carefully peering out the window. The morning sun burned her blue eyes. Squinting, she gazed down the main street where she'd walked from. The street was humming with folks passing by the storefronts. A Clydesdale clip-clopped along the pavement, pulling a red and black carriage filled with excited shoppers. In the distance, a green car was parked in front of the crawfish shack. Holly had stayed there one night and ate leftover *low country boil* in the middle of the night. She had been thankful, but she was far more comfortable now in the cottage. She had needed the rest and nourishment she'd received in just one night there.

Stepping back from the window, Holly went to the restroom before returning and taking a peek out the window by the front door. The house directly across the street had a car in the driveway. She couldn't remember seeing it the night before, but she'd been too busy rehearsing her plea should someone have been in the cottage. She briefly wondered how she'd managed to land in this particular house, which was furnished with everything she happened to need.

After a breakfast of eggs, toast, and a cup of hot coffee, Holly cleaned up the dishes. Grandpa had told her that drinking coffee wouldn't harm her baby, so she maintained a cup or two each day, for her own comfort. Taking her warm mug with her, she went into the bathroom and dressed herself in the only clean outfit she had left in her satchel. Then, she combed through her long straight hair before carrying her backpack out of the bathroom and around the corner to the small area that housed the washing machine and dryer.

The cabinet hanging above the appliances contained several bottles of laundry detergent. Holly grabbed one and began filling the washer with hot soapy water before tossing in every stitch of her dirty laundry. The bag felt mostly empty without all of her clothes in it, although it was only a couple of outfits, socks, and underwear.

As the washing machine did its work with a soft rumble, Holly took the ceramic coffee mug and paced softly across the carpeted floor toward the unmade bed.

She wondered if it would be safe to run the dryer. If any neighbors were assigned to watch out for the cottage, might they notice the steam created by the exhaust in the winter's air?

Before she could concern herself very much with the decision, her mind shifted to something more important…something she hadn't thought about before. For the first time, Holly became nervous about the coming of the baby.

Her stomach lurched at the same moment the baby offered a hearty kick in the ribs. Holly looked down and cradled her large, round stomach with her dark green T-shirt stretched over it. It can't be much longer, now, she thought.

It had been ten months since Colt shoved her into the empty barn stall and had his disgusting way with her. She remembered the day well, though she tried her best not to. Now, there were more important things to worry about. What would she do? Where would she and the baby go? It wasn't safe back home, and Holly knew she'd need to protect the baby.

Colt didn't know Holly had gotten pregnant. He wouldn't find out either, if she could help it. She had stayed indoors as much as possible over the last several months. Not only was it important to hide her pregnant belly, but Grandpa also insisted that she go nowhere near Colt. He said he didn't want to risk the chance of Holly running into that imbecile again. Grandpa was willing to protect Holly at all costs. He'd kept saying "he's going to get what's coming to him one of these days…"

Though Holly wasn't exactly sure what he'd really meant by that, Grandpa left her alone to wonder if he'd gotten himself hurt while trying to defend her. The thought made Holly's head spin and her heart ache. She knew she'd never forget the night the police knocked on the door of her familiar old cabin and gently told her that her Grandpa had been found dead.

He had been found lying face down on the side of the road next to his truck, about two miles down the road. It appeared that a head injury had been what killed him. Holly could think of no explanation as to why Grandpa would've parked his truck on the side of the road and gotten out. But what she did think of was that Grandpa was found less than a mile from Colt's house.

The night that Holly fled Tennessee further validated Holly's suspicions when those cold words mixed with the smell of beer spilled out of his nasty mouth.

Try and run from me, and you'll end up dead, just like your grandpa.

He was so drunk, and Holly had on such baggy clothing that he never even noticed she was pregnant. He'd crept up the driveway, his headlights turned off, and barged in the front door. Holly was sure she'd locked it–she always locked the doors for fear of him. But she'd apparently been mistaken that night, and she realized it too late.

It was a wonder to Holly how the fear that came over her hadn't harmed the baby when she saw Colt stumbling toward her. She just knew he was going to hurt her. She knew he'd find out she was pregnant, and there was no telling what he'd do then.

Miraculously, Colt didn't hurt her. He barely even had the strength to stand; otherwise, he would've. Instead, he swayed back and forth as he inched closer to her in the small kitchen. She had backed as far away from him as she could, her back pressed against the porcelain sink.

Strangely, he, in his stupor, just fumbled around until he managed to grasp her hair. He made his weak threats and stumbled back out the front door toward his truck. Holly never said a word. Though her heart was racing, she managed to control her fear lest it control her. She quickly locked the door before checking the rest of the doors in the house. Then, she watched out the darkened window as Colt left recklessly in his dirty old truck.

Quickly, Holly gathered the things she'd brought with her to the little cottage on the South Carolina coast. Her mind snapped back to the present as she felt another jolt from the baby. She smiled, briefly, wondering who the baby would be. It didn't matter to her how he or she had been conceived. Though she was unsure of everything else, one thing she was certain of was that she'd always love and protect the child within her. After all, the baby was all she had.

Taking her lukewarm cup of coffee with her to the bedside, Holly admired the worn, antique piece of furniture on which the lamp sat. The white paint had cracked and chipped away, revealing a contrasting dark wood beneath it. A single drawer with a tiny, amber-colored knob begged to be opened. Placing her mug on the little table, Holly slowly pulled on the cool glass knob and peeked inside the small drawer.

Inside was a single spiral notebook. Picking it up, Holly admired the mountain scene printed on the cover. It reminded her of home with its crooked creek etched into the hills and the orange sunset streaking the sky. Bringing it to her lap, Holly opened the attractive cover to reveal a feminine handwriting on the first page. She pulled the chain, turning on the lamp, and settled back onto the fluffy pillows as she began to read.

THREE

I don't even know where to begin... I've never journaled before. Though I've wanted to, I just never could seem to find the time. My life has just been so full. And busy. And wonderful. I'd like to write down some of the things that have made it so grand; after all, a diary changed my life many years ago.

Addie was married last month. She married a wonderful young man named Paul, who will love, honor, and protect her until death. I'm so very thankful that my Addie found him. I'm also thankful for my other two sons-in-law. Each of them is a man I would have hand-picked for my daughters myself.

My last baby, though not a baby anymore, is Aaron. At twenty years old, he's a lot of help to us around the farm–especially to Joseph. Still, we'd like to see him married to a lovely woman in the near future. I believe Joseph and I have raised our children to wisely choose a spouse, and I suppose Aaron just hasn't found the right woman yet.

I can remember vividly the day he came into this

world. I remember the births of all of my babies well…and very fondly. Each of them was born here, in my house. In the house I grew up in and will likely die in.

Oh, the things these scuffed walls have seen.

Sometimes, I can still see Grandmama over by the stove even after all these years. She'd be wiping her hands on her pink apron and muttering something under her breath. She always talked to herself in the kitchen.

I can still see Daddy sitting at the dining table, drinking his coffee as he held the newspaper in a calloused, outstretched hand. He winks at me from behind his reading glasses as I enter the room.

Though the sting of Daddy's departure has lessened over the years, my love for him hasn't. I still miss him. I still wish he were here. But there's no ache in my heart for him any longer, and there hasn't been for a long time.

Daddy hadn't been gone very long when I stumbled upon Old Addie's diary in an old nightstand I bought at an antique store. We call her Old Addie – she's not here to object, but I don't think she would anyway. I think she'd be delighted to have a namesake like my lovely newly married daughter.

Old Addie's words captivated me right away. They changed the way I looked at life, which had been depressingly monotonous up until then. I wanted so badly to find the mysterious, wise woman I'd come to know through her lost diary. But between my job as a nurse, my newfound beau (Joseph), and the house I'd just bought and was trying to get moved into, I wasn't able to pursue a genuine search for Old Addie.

I found her, though. In the most unexpected turn my life had taken up until then, I found that Old Addie was not only the same Ms. Adelaide that had been one of my patients at the nursing home, but I also learned that she had lived in the home that I was just moving into. I think back on those few days surrounding the shocking discoveries, and I'm thankful that they're part of me. However, when you've lived a life as rich as mine, you've felt every emotion there is to feel. Some more powerful, but never dulling the many others that have penetrated my soul at some time or another.

After I married Joseph, shortly after moving into Old Addie's farmhouse, I met someone else who changed my life in a wonderful way...my sister, Violet. I never knew I had a sister, and neither did she. But as we became friends and talked about the person that tied us together by a common thread...Old Addie revealed to us in her diary that Violet and I shared a father. Another deeply emotional experience I've tucked into my pocket.

I still remember the special day vividly. I was able to maintain my composure as I walked to Violet's van. She was picking me up for a trip to her beach cottage (that she'd inherited from her mother, Madge–Old Addie's closest friend). I had only discovered the truth that Old Addie had written about Violet and me, the night before our scheduled trip. I don't know how I resisted the impulse to call her right away, but I did. I lay in a sort of shock, staring at the ceiling from my bed, trying to fathom what I'd just learned. My heart raced as I thought of Daddy, and Violet, and how my wonderful childhood could've been even better had it been spent with her.

The next morning, a bit light-headed, I calmly got into the passenger seat of Violet's van with a duffel bag on my shoulder. I handed the diary to her, which I had opened to the correct page. 'Read this,' was all I said. And then I sat and waited, while I studied her face. For the first time, as she read, I noticed that she had our father's lips and his dimpled chin.

Violet dropped the open diary onto her lap, her stare piercing me like a dagger. Her red lip quivered as her eyes became glassy.

For a long moment, we just sat and stared at one another in silence. Neither of us had any words, yet we each knew how the other felt.

Finally, Violet leaned over and embraced me with both of her shaky arms. I held onto her as my own tears fell and dampened her shoulder. I can still remember the feel of her soft knit sweater and the smell of her damp, red hair.

From that moment on, we've been inseparable. I guess you could say we've done our best to make up for the lost time. I love Violet so very much. I can't imagine my life without her in it.

Shortly after she and I discovered that we were sisters, I found out that my abandoned childhood home was for sale by the new owners—a timely, unlikely surprise. With little persuading of Joseph, we made an offer right away. Though I loved the home Old Addie had lived in before me, my heart longed to be inside my childhood home. The whole reason I fell for Old Addie's house in the first place was because of its resemblance to my old home. But it wasn't and couldn't ever be the same.

As soon as our offer was accepted, Violet and her husband, John, made us an offer on Old Addie's house. The home meant something to Violet. too, since she spent a considerable amount of time there as a child with her mother, visiting Old Addie.

Over the years, Violet and I have graced the doorways of each other's homes more times than we could ever count. At some point early on, we stopped knocking when we'd enter each other's house. We just go on in, usually carrying a borrowed dish or a hot meal to share. I guess you could say we both sort of have two homes, though she'd agree...one of them is perfect, and the other is near-perfect. We'd disagree on which one was which, but we'd both be right.

I am beyond grateful that we were able to raise our children together. Though a few of hers are a good bit older than mine, some have overlapped, and we even have two children each who are within a month of the same age.

These days, I find myself slowing down considerably, and I often feel at a loss for what to do with my time. Of course, I still cook every meal at home as I always did, except it's only Joseph, Aaron, and me now. Slowly, the number gathered around our dining table has dwindled closer to two, as it began. It's not as dramatic as if the number had changed suddenly, but sometimes, with some effort, I can picture them all there. Giggles, prayers, spilled cups of milk, homeschool lessons, tantrums...this house –this dining room–has seen it all.

Violet was here today. She brought me a basket full of okra from her garden and returned my bread basket. We have plans to head down to the beach cottage in a few days. Nowadays, it's just Violet and me when we travel there. We spend our time at the South Carolina coast slow and nonchalant, reminiscing with laughter and grateful hearts. We eat low-country seafood, collect bits of sea glass and shells, and enjoy the smell of salt and coconut-scented tanning oil.

Joseph and Aaron hold down the fort now while Violet and I are away on our little trips. When I return next week, I expect they'll have the rest of the firewood split for the winter, the cattle will have been moved to a fresh paddock of lush forage, hogs will have been sent to the market, and the refrigerator will be piled with the vegetables from the garden, minus the ones they will give to friends and neighbors.

Joseph is very gentle, yet very strong. He's always taken care of the needs of the entire family without complaint, and without ever objecting to any notion I've taken, such as taking off to the beach with my sister while the men fend for themselves. I suspect the two of them will have some fun when the work is all done. They'll probably eat greasy cheeseburgers for supper and hang around the cattle auction until late at night.

Aaron, my youngest boy...is so much like his father. Gentle and strong. Intuitive and humorous. Friendly and kind. I can't wait to meet the woman he chooses for his wife. I know without a doubt that she will be one of a kind.

I suppose I've written enough for my very first journal entry. It has been soothing to reminisce a bit. Violet and I will leave at dawn. I'll take this diary along with me and write from the beach cottage. I can already hear the sound of the waves crashing in the early morning hours as I sip my coffee from the porch.

Until next time,

Blaire

FOUR

As she lowered the diary to her lap, Holly sighed with a bit of relief at the realization that she was indeed currently lodging in a vacation home. With it being only a few days before Christmas, she was sure nobody would be visiting the beach house. Holly smiled, a faint trickle as she lay her head back on the pillow behind her. The baby pressed its foot into her ribs and kept it there, but she didn't mind.

Holly was intrigued by Blaire; she wondered how far away she lived, what she looked like…She sure seemed to have a pleasant and peaceful life. Laying the opened diary aside, Holly reached toward the bedside table and retrieved her coffee mug. It wasn't very hot anymore, but it was comforting nevertheless. The homey smell of the fresh coffee brewing still lingered in the air, just like it did back at home every morning and evening. As she took a sip, Holly wondered how long it took for Blaire's aching heart to heal after her father had passed away. It seemed as if Holly's heart would never stop aching for her Grandpa.

Much like the way Blaire could so easily picture her Daddy sitting at the dining table reading the newspaper, Holly could blink, and Grandpa's smiling face was there. So familiar, so comforting. But so incredibly lonesome, because she knew that he wasn't really there. She was alone, and she wondered how long she would be. She could stay in the beach house and munch away at the food until either it ran out or someone came and found her there.

And then what? Where would she and the baby go, and how would they get there? Holly wasn't sure of much of anything as of late. But, she knew it would be okay. She felt safe in the beach cottage. At least she had a warm home to give birth in when the time came. She would just have to take things one day at a time. Or one hour at a time, rather.

Holly's stomach lurched again. It wasn't the baby wiggling, but her own butterflies of nervousness. The thought of the baby being born scared her. If she were at home with Grandpa, she wouldn't be scared. He'd know what to do – or who to call upon. Though he didn't believe it to be absolutely necessary to have Holly seen for routine doctor visits, he had insisted that she take a spoonful of blackstrap molasses each day, along with the special fish oil pills that he got from the drugstore. He also saw that she ate a daily handful of fresh kale from the winter garden if she could. The greens tasted so good to Holly, whether fresh or cooked. Grandpa had said that if she really had a hankering for anything, then that was a sign that her body needed it.

Grandpa knew lots of things about lots of things. It came from being the oldest of ten children, growing up in the midst of the Great Depression. It seemed that he never ran out of stories to tell about his young life. As an adult, he met and married Holly's Grandmother (Grandma Sue). Holly remembered Grandma Sue fondly, but the memories were faint and few, since she passed away when Holly was only seven years old.

Somewhere between the time that Grandpa took custody of Holly after her parents dropped her off with him and left, he met Miss Agnes. She was a prim and proper southern lady if ever there was one. She wore a wide-brimmed hat to church on Sundays, pearls, and pink lipstick always. She kept her white hair perfectly shellacked with strong, sweet-smelling hairspray. And she came over every Saturday night, bringing a tray full of homemade chocolate cream puffs.

After she'd had supper with Grandpa and Holly, she would share the tray of light, delectable desserts with them as they giggled happily around the table. Then, she'd help Holly clear the table and clean the dishes. Miss Agnes never let on at church or in public whatsoever that she was a friend of Grandpa's, but Holly knew that it was she who called late at night, nearly every night of the week. As she lay in bed upstairs, Holly could hear Grandpa mumbling from his chair by the phone in the hallway.

Though a majority of the rest of the world had the internet and cell phones, Grandpa was different. He didn't care one bit for "newfangled" technology. They had a small television in the living room, a radio in the kitchen, and the landline phone with a long cord in the hallway.

Holly wouldn't have changed the way things were, even if she could have. She was perfectly content with her books, drawing pads, and the landline phone she used to talk with her girlfriends on.

Holly wondered if any of her old friends were worried about her. Katrina came to visit her one day, closely following Grandpa's passing. She sat with her for a long time, and though she didn't say anything, Holly supposed she knew about the pregnancy. It was really getting difficult by then to conceal her large belly, even with the roomy housecoat she'd thrown on when she saw Katrina's car coming up the long driveway toward the house.

Between Katrina, Miss Agnes, and a few others, Holly wondered if there would be any 'missing persons' report filed regarding her. If there were, her face would be plastered all over the news stations and everywhere else, she thought. It was best, she knew, that she stayed right where she was, with the world outside locked out. She wasn't sure when she'd see the light of day again, and she didn't feel much like worrying about that. A strong squeeze came about her belly as soon as she stood from the bed. She had not felt a sensation quite like that before, and it made her heart pick up the pace.

The squeeze lasted only a few seconds, low underneath her round belly. It felt like a string was pulling on her lower abdominal muscles, stitching her up. When it had passed, Holly took a deep breath and rubbed her belly where the 'stitch' had been. Then she carried her coffee mug to the kitchen, where she washed and rinsed it.

Though the stitch wasn't all that painful, it got her attention and made her feel afraid of what was to come. She decided to keep her mind as busy as possible, which wasn't very easy in a small, tidy home. She took the wet clothes out of the washing machine and tossed them into the dryer before padding softly through the bedroom. Holly walked over to the window nearest the bed. Cracking the blinds ever so slightly, she surveyed the street as far as she could see. There wasn't much to observe other than the rain that was beginning to fall. Homes on either side of the street were aglow both with Christmas lights and through the golden windows. Holly had continued to use only small lamps inside the cottage, so as not to cause any concern from potential meddling neighbors.

Stepping away from the window, she settled back onto the soft bed and picked up the diary again. Flipping through a bit, she could see that the same feminine handwriting covered the pages on about half of the notebook. She picked up where she'd left off.

Maybe she'd find out more about Blaire and Violet as written from perhaps right in the very same spot on the bed. She opened the diary as she lay down on her left side and propped herself on her elbow in front of it. The baby rolled over.

FIVE

For nearly the entire drive down to the beach cottage, I thought about the births of my four babies. I'm not even quite sure what sparked the thought, but once I began thinking of the miraculous events, I couldn't stop thinking about them. After all, they have been the most wonderful moments of my life thus far.

I thought that while the miracle of birth was on the forefront of my mind, and I had some moments at hand of quiet concentration with the sounds of the waves crashing and the seagulls calling, I would write these down from the small porch of the beach cottage. Whether they will ever be read by anyone other than me, I have no idea. But I simply cannot bear for them to be forgotten. At least this way, my stories have a chance to live on. Maybe my own daughters, or granddaughters will read the stories of the day they, or their family members, came into this world. Maybe this will serve as a sort of comfort for them in the unknown territory of birthing the firstborn child.

I'll start with the birth of Aaron, since he is the

youngest and therefore his birth is slightly fresher in my mind– as much as it can be, to have happened twenty years ago!

Of course, I had entrusted Violet to be my honorary midwife, as I had with all the rest of my babies. Though she had never had any official training or education regarding birth, I was satisfied that she was experienced enough to care for my pregnancies and confidently preside over my births, given that she'd birthed many children in the safety of her own home.

Violet's mother, Madge, was well versed in childbirth, as well. Her best friend was Old Addie, and Old Addie was a well-seasoned midwife herself. Indulging in the many diaries she had left behind in her old house, I was able to experience through the reading of her elegant handwriting, the wonderful miracle of birth, as told by Old Addie. That is where the fascination of childbirth began for me. I learned so much from her that I decided long before I had children that I wanted to someday give birth to them in the comfort of my own home. And I did... all four of them.

Aaron was born at Christmastime...my favorite time of year since first becoming a mother, many years ago. I had always enjoyed the Christmas season as a child, but my love for it boldly intensified when I finally had my own family to share it with. The Decembers we've spent around the fire and in our small farmhouse kitchen have created memories that will remain with me forevermore.

I was "due" on December 10th, though I have never believed in giving my babies the infamous eviction notice. I assumed the baby would come at least one week past that date, and he proved me right.

On the morning of December 19th, my three girls and I made breakfast together, as we did many mornings. Addie wanted to make omelettes, Maeve wanted waffles, and Sarah had a fierce craving for some of our homemade yogurt with frozen blueberries. So, we had all three – a breakfast feast for all! Joseph had slept in, being tired from having worked three twelve-hour shifts at the police department. By the time he stumbled into the kitchen, we were just getting the food on the table, and the coffee was brewing.

I remember being unusually tired that morning, although I had had a full night's sleep. Joseph leaned over my large belly between us and kissed my forehead.

After breakfast, Sarah and Maeve helped me clear away the table and wash up the dishes, while little Addie went into her bedroom to feed her baby doll.

The house was fully decked in holiday trimmings. With Joseph's help, I had decorated the inside and out weeks prior. The slender white porch columns were wrapped in greenery with a fresh cedar wreath on the front door and flickering candlelights in all of the windows.

Inside, there were garlands of dried oranges, cranberries, and homemade gingerbread dough boys strung above the windows and around the full, glowing

Christmas tree. Ribbons and bells and candles adorned the interior of our country home. Bluegrass Christmas tunes played through static from my small kitchen radio that sat on the countertop. The delicious aroma of molasses and cloves filled the house as I pulled two large pans of homemade gingersnap cookies out of the oven.

At the end of each of my pregnancies with the girls, I always had the habit of baking some sort of wholesome and comforting treat to enjoy in the days following the birth. One of my favorite delights I've had the privilege of experiencing in all my life is lying in bed holding a tiny newborn while indulging in a warm homemade treat. That particular year, I thought it fitting to prepare my favorite soft gingersnap cookies as the 'postpartum reward', since it happened to be surrounding the Christmas holiday.

The girls, Joseph, and I each snuck a cookie or two while they were still warm from the oven. I had planned to take the rest of them and stash them in the freezer until they were needed; I knew Joseph could re-warm them for us later, after the baby had been born.

But I did not freeze the cookies. Instead, I wrapped them in a pretty Christmas tea towel and then placed them in the snowman cookie jar on the counter. Something told me that preserving the baked goods would not be necessary. That something was the first 'real' contraction of my labor with baby Aaron.

Having already had three babies before, I had

learned very well the difference between 'practice contractions' and the beginning of active labor. Each of my labors began the same way, moved relatively quickly, and produced for me a very healthy baby. The tightening in the very lowermost part of my belly grew tighter and became closer together in frequency, telling me that it was going to be the baby's birthday.

Even with the fourth baby, my heart rate quickened for just a moment, a little bit of nervousness, along with the excitement that always comes with a newborn. I remember checking the clock at 9:09 a.m. I hurriedly wiped the countertops, table, and stove, and then I went over the kitchen and dining area with the broom.

Everything else was already done. There were fresh loaves of homemade sourdough bread in the freezer – I went ahead and retrieved one of them at that time, and placed it on the kitchen counter next to the cookie jar. Cinnamon rolls and soups were made ahead and frozen as well. The cinnamon rolls were prepared ahead of time for the special Christmas Eve breakfast tradition. I would have Joseph bake them for us on that very special morning. The bed linens were fresh and clean. The laundry was caught up on. The gifts were all wrapped. The baby's things were laundered and readily available in a wicker basket –he wouldn't need much...just a few gowns, diapers, and powder. Christmastime nesting was ultra-satisfying, and I mentally referred to myself as a partridge nesting in a pear tree.

As I was tying up the loose ends of the morning, I happened to glance up at our beautiful Christmas tree, which stood in the corner of the living room by the staircase and was visible from the dining table. The large red ornament hung near the top of the tree, which read 'JOY'. It was very fitting, as I felt pure joy on that December morning.

"Girls," I'd said as they skipped around the kitchen, nibbling their cookies. "Is Daddy gone out to give the cows their hay?"

"Yes, Mama," Sarah had answered. "Why did you ask?" she asked with such genuine curiosity.

"Well, I just had some pains right here..." I rubbed my large, tight belly. "I'm okay...I just wanted to let him know that the baby might be coming soon!"

I said this excitedly to the girls, with a smile that mirrored theirs.

"The baby is coming! The baby is coming!" Maeve jumped up and down while Sarah ran to the door and peered out the fogged window through the misty rain that was falling outside.

"Don't go worrying Daddy, now. It's okay...he'll be back inside in just a few minutes." I told them assuredly.

Sure enough, Joseph was back inside in just a short while, with all three girls bouncing around him as he pulled his barn boots off and left them on the rug by the door.

"Daddy, Mama's baby is coming!" Maeve chanted

as the other girls squealed.

Joseph widened his eyes and looked straight at me with a bit of perplexity in his stare. Then his face quickly cracked into a soft, happy expression that he could not disguise for another second.

"Well...I think so!" I answered his unasked question. I rubbed my hand back and forth along the bottom of my large belly as another contraction came.

By the fourth child, Joseph pretty much knew what he could expect. He knew, of course, that the labor was just beginning and that we had some time–but not very much! My labors always progressed fairly quickly, and thankfully, I had never had any stallings or complications.

"Have you called Violet?" Joseph asked as he walked toward me.

"No. Not yet," I answered. "It just started. I've only had a few contractions so far, but I know it's starting."

"Well, just remember...Addie was born after just two hours, and Violet almost didn't make it here in time. Just don't wait too late," he'd warned.

Though he was familiar with the process of birth, he always expressed a strong desire to have someone else present who could help in case of an emergency. I always teased him about that, saying he was just squeamish.

"Don't worry, I'll call her soon," I assured Joseph as I scooped little Addie up into my arms. "Come on,

you sweetie girl. Let's go get the coffee ready for Aunt Violet."

As I carried her in my arms, I briefly mourned the fleeting moments that brought her nearer to being a big sister, rather than my baby. It happened with all of my girls each time I was in labor. I'd begin to get emotional just looking at their little faces, knowing that another precious little one would soon join them. I was always very grateful that they each handled the adjustment of a new baby with excitement and ease. Not a single one of them ever became jealous when I had a new baby...only innocently curious and adoring of the tiny addition.

I called Violet and told her that my labor had begun about thirty minutes prior. Of course, she knew my history and the nature of my typical labor and delivery, having been the one to deliver each one of my babies...though Violet – like Old Addie– objected to using the term "delivered". They insisted that the mother delivers the baby; the midwife only assists. I always just chuckled and went along with them.

Violet arrived very shortly after I had called her, carrying her bag full of birth supplies and a large thermos full of something I was not sure of. By the time she had arrived, which was only an hour after my labor had first begun, the contractions were coming quickly and were growing fairly intense. I could still walk and talk through each one, but it was getting more and more difficult to do so with each passing one. I knew that it probably would not be very long before the baby would arrive. Though I had no reason to anticipate the labor being drawn out very long, I walked over to the kitchen cupboard and retrieved a jar of honey before enjoying a sweet spoonful of it. I had learned to do that from Old Addie's diary, where she talked about keeping honey on hand for laboring mothers to snack on. She had written that it helped to keep their energy levels up for the labor and delivery, and was a quick and easy source of nutrients. I was sure to adopt the habit into my laboring and birthing practices from the first one. If for no other reason than because Old Addie said so.

I lay on the couch in between contractions, listening to the pops and crackles of the logs in the Fisher wood stove. When another surge would come, I would find myself on my knees, rocking back and forth as I braced myself with my arms on the back of the couch. Sweat droplets dripped down my back with each contraction as Violet placed ice-cold washcloths on my forehead. In between them, I was comfortable and calm, resting up for the next one.

Joseph stayed close by, and as far as I can recall, the girls stayed quiet. I can't remember them making any kind of noise that bothered me. Violet pushed the washcloth against my lower back with each contraction that I had. She and I both knew that I was in the thick of the hardest part of labor. With each powerful wave, I groaned from the lowest part of my being. Partly because I'd memorized the trick Violet taught me with my very first labor – to groan low and deep in order to relax the lower muscles and help the baby down. And partly because my body was beginning to grunt and push on its own. It is difficult to explain to anyone who has not experienced it for themselves.

After that point, I lost sense of time and everything else around me. It was the portion of labor that I always seemed to take leave of myself. I was there, physically, but it felt as though I was being propelled into another world with each contraction's peak. As it slowly fell, I began to slowly return to the present world.

There were not very many of that type of surge, thankfully. I am not sure how long I was in the phase of transitioning to the pushing part, but I believe it was only about fifteen minutes or so, and for that, I was very grateful. Soon, I felt that wonderful urge to push – the relieving sign that the hard work was over. Though it burned like a branding iron as the baby descended, I really didn't mind too much. I tried to be patient and refrain from forcing the baby out through intentional pushes, but I have always found refraining to be extremely difficult. So, with each powerful squeeze from my womb, I bore down with all my might as the baby crawled downward.

First the head, then almost immediately the body followed. My brand new baby was earth-side at last. As soon as Violet caught him, I crumpled to the couch, which had been lined with towels without my noticing. I immediately took the baby from Violet's hands as she held him against my chest. His warm, slick body was tiny and gray in my hands. As I rubbed his little chest, his first cry sounded like sweet music to my ears. A little gurgly at first, it grew louder, clearer, and more precious.

I brought him back to my chest and shushed and rubbed his slippery back. His wet hair was light in color but plentiful. I crumbled into the couch as I experienced the complete euphoria that only comes with holding your newborn baby for the very first time. I could never write an adequate description of those poignant moments. Though the first moments are fleeting, the memories are so deep within me that I can close my eyes now and go right back there. I don't know of any other memory so influential that it is able to penetrate the soul in such a vivid way.

Joseph cradled both the baby and me, and a smile of pure adoration spread across his tear-streaked face. Finally, after a few sacred moments, we agreed that it was time to check the baby's gender. We were surprised and eager to discover the gender at the time of the birth. As I held the baby out at arm's length, we all laughed with joy at the sight of our first son.

Joy, pure joy, is the only word I have to describe the seconds, hours, and days following the birth of a new baby. Even the smell of birth, for me, provides comfort and familiarity, intertwined with the aroma of lavender and peppermint from the herbal soaks Violet always prepared for my healing bottom.

As I lay back on the soft sofa, wrapped in flannel blankets with baby Aaron on my chest, Violet checked me for tearing and bleeding. Everything was wonderfully, perfectly normal. Joseph and our little girls surrounded baby Aaron and me as I relished in the pure bliss of holding my family close. The fire crackled in the nearby woodstove, offering radiant warmth and luxurious comfort. Joseph served me with utmost diligence, delivering warmed soups, toasted bread, tea, and of course, my gingersnap cookies to my heart's content. The few weeks spent with the cocooned newborn were absolutely remarkable. Because of our farming lifestyle, it was always difficult to leave for very many vacations; so, Joseph always saved up his vacation time to use during my postpartum periods.

Christmas came and went during those blissful days. It was one to be remembered by all of us (minus Aaron, but he's heard the story many times). I celebrated the special holiday mostly from my worn, comfortable place on the couch with the six-day-old infant in my arms, or on my chest. He slept both night and day, waking only to nurse. I sat for hours watching his precious facial expressions, taking in every second of the sacred newborn bliss. The girls spent time in the living room with us, as well as with Joseph outside. He took them along with him to perform their favorite chore...milking Molly, our Jersey cow. That was ordinarily my responsibility, and I took it seriously up until the day I gave birth–then, it was Joseph's turn to take over, and he did it with gladness.

The girls and I watched Little Women on television, read books, took turns holding Aaron, and colored pictures together. I talked Joseph through a couple of simple meals I'd prepped in the days before the baby had come. On Christmas Eve, I was thankful I had made that dish of cinnamon rolls ahead of time and tucked them away in the deep freezer. Joseph baked them for us to have with mugs full of Molly's fresh, creamy milk. The house smelled heavenly as the cinnamon rolls browned to perfection in the oven. They ought to have, what with the two cups of butter that they contained!

On Christmas Day, Violet and the whole family burst through the front door, each of them carrying a dish of some kind. Then they all trekked back to the van and returned, each carrying gifts. Violet and her oldest daughters had prepared a feast to share with us. A baked ham, candied carrots, cranberry sauce, herbed potatoes, pies, fudge, and even mulled holiday cider, which two of the children carried in plastic milk jugs while Violet searched my shelves for my brass punch bowl.

I sat in overwhelming joy at the splendor of the table all set, lined with food and glowing red and green candlesticks. The children ran around the room, giggling and talking, the twinkling of the Christmas tree lights matching the twinkle in their little eyes. Joseph and I had agreed to be satisfied with a more relaxed Christmas that year. I had wrapped the girls' gifts weeks before and placed them beneath the large tree. We had planned to have my pre-prepared potato soup with sourdough bread and 'Molly-milk-cocoa'. I was more than happy with that vision of Christmas –after all, I was holding a newborn nearly every second of my favorite holiday season–how could I be less than jubilant?

But my heart nearly burst with joy at the feasting with Violet and her family on that Christmas Day. It is a day I will hold dear in my heart for as long as I live… maybe even longer.

If my dear daughters ever read this: Your birth stories are stored away in the most special corners of my heart, as well. I will write them down for you to read, if you wish. None is more special than the other, though each differ in some way. I still dream of the days when all of you were tiny babies, sleeping softly in my arms. I know without a doubt that if my memory ever fails me as a result of old age, I will still continue to go there in my dreams, time after time.

Love, Blaire

SIX

Holly smiled as she closed the diary and laid it on the bed beside her. As she rubbed her large, round belly, the anxiety melted away and was replaced by a surge of excitement. How fitting, she thought, that she would read a true story about the happiness of birth when she most needed assurance. Blaire's point of view offered comfort, and Holly suddenly knew that she could do it.

Rising from the bed, Holly headed for the kitchen where she began opening cabinet doors. "I know I saw flour in here somewhere," she said aloud as she rummaged through the fully stocked cupboard. Tucked in the midst of the baking needs, Holly found the tub of flour. She reached for it along with a container of baking soda and some cinnamon. Surely Blaire had left some ginger in here, too…

Finally, Holly located all the ingredients she thought she'd need, and she proceeded to create her very own postpartum gingersnap reward. Though it wouldn't be quite the comforting experience that Blaire had written about, it would be the best it could possibly be, given the circumstances. After all, Holly thought, at least she was safe away from Colt. He would never be able to find her here. She was sure of that.

As she busied herself around the comfortable little kitchen, a tightening came, making her pause from her task of sweeping the flour-sprinkled floor. She stood upright and danced back and forth until the tightening was over.

The cottage began to fill with the sweet aroma of the gingersnap cookies that were baking. Holly looked at the clock hanging above the antique baker's cabinet. She'd had a tightening five minutes ago, which was at 1:05 p.m. She decided she'd start keeping track of them, just in case.

Opening each cabinet door, Holly searched for what she knew would surely be there somewhere. As the dark brown cookies cooled on the stovetop, Holly retrieved the jar from the cabinet. She set the clear glass jar full of honey and honeycomb out on the countertop before laying a tablespoon next to it.

The phrase "partridge nesting in a pear tree" came to mind and brought a smile to Holly's lips as she went into the small bathroom to retrieve towels and washcloths. Laying them on the chest by the foot of the bed, she crossed the dim room again and paced back and forth across the kitchen. She wasn't sure what else she should do…she wasn't sure if there was anything at all she *could* do, other than wait.

She didn't have any baby clothes, diapers, or even a baby blanket, but she wasn't worried. She knew everything would be all right; it had to be, didn't it?

There were no dirty clothes or linens to be washed, and the house had plenty of towels, washcloths and dish towels. She would make do with those – it wouldn't be too difficult to toss them into the washing machine when she started running low.

Another tightening came across her lower abdomen. This time, it seemed to be more powerful. It lasted longer, too. Holly placed both of her hands on the kitchen counter and took a deep breath as the tightening slowly released. She relaxed and glanced up at the clock. It was 1:10.

"That was only five minutes," she whispered, her heart rate accelerating.

Looking around the kitchen, she dabbed at her brow with the back of her hand before straightening her back and continuing her tasks. She took a thin green tea towel from the drawer by the sink and draped it over the pan of cooling cookies.

"Soup…I need to make some soup," she uttered, spinning around to retrieve a large pot from where it hung over the butcherblock island. Though Holly had never been in labor before, she felt that there was not an excess of time. A homemade soup would be healthier, but canned soup would do nicely, and she knew there was plenty of it in the pantry. She paced the few steps over to the large closet and stepped inside. She scanned the selection before her, deciding on the chicken noodle. There were five cans, which she took, carrying them in her arms and setting them on the counter.

She poured each can of soup into the large pot and turned the stove on *low* so that the soup could simmer slowly. Then, to make it go further, she added a couple of cans of water to the pot. She would have plenty of soup, as she needed it. She felt satisfied knowing that the next several meals were essentially prepared.

"Okay, soup's done...what else?" She looked around the kitchen as she tried to think clearly.

Before she could decide what she should get going next, another tightening began. Climbing in intensity, Holly thought it had lasted longer than the one before. She took several long, deep breaths throughout the duration of the contraction. Then, she looked up at the clock. Right on schedule, she thought. The clock read 1:15.

It certainly didn't seem that there would be enough time to make homemade bread, as Blaire had done. Although Holly knew how to make bread, and the ingredients were probably close at hand, she decided she had better save up her energy. Walking back to the pantry, she scanned the shelves until she found a box of saltine crackers.

"These will do," she said aloud as she placed the unopened box of crackers on the counter next to the jar of honey. Then, she sifted through the variety of tea bags that were in a woven basket on the counter. She grabbed two packets of chamomile tea and dropped both of them into a green pottery mug, hanging the string over the rim.

The water in the tea kettle began to heat up as Holly leaned over the counter, rocking her hips back and forth in time to another contraction. They were growing stronger; there was no doubt about it.

The tea kettle began to whistle as steam escaped the spout. Holly poured the hot water over the tea bags, leaving the tea to steep while she left the kitchen in search of some blankets. The chest by the foot of the bed seemed to be a good place to store such things, so Holly checked there first. By the light of the lamp on the dresser, she could see there were folded quilts, soft, plush afghans, extra sheets, and pillow cases.

Carefully sifting through the linens, Holly selected the softest material she could find. Holding it up, she unfolded the pastel yellow fabric to discover a perfectly-sized baby blanket that smelled of cedar. This is perfect, she thought, as she laid it aside. She took an extra set of forest-green sheets and laid them on the dresser with the baby blanket before closing the wooden chest.

Back in the small kitchen, Holly sifted through the drawers – she was sure she'd seen a box of matches in one of the drawers before. Among the batteries and Sharpie markers, Holly found the small box of matches. She took them and walked through the small cottage, lighting every candle she could see. Blaire and Violet must have been fond of candles; there were two or three in each room, varying in color and fragrance.

The contractions continued, becoming strong enough to momentarily debilitate Holly. She slowly dropped to the floor and rocked her body back and forth throughout the duration of the intense spasm of her womb. The belt of pain circled around to her back with each contraction, worsening the pain. She hadn't prepared herself for that, but she assumed it was all normal and part of the process.

She wondered just how long the process would be. Her mind flashed to Blaire's story of Aaron's birth. She had written about how wonderful it all was – Holly was sure she had not reached the wonderful part yet. However, she looked forward to it with a yearning hope. As sweat ran down her back, she quickly slipped her shirt over her head before pushing her jogging pants off her hips and ripping them off her feet. Another pain was coming. She felt it building as it grew in strength. She began to groan deeply, the way Blaire had talked about. The low, shaky moans began to come out involuntarily.

The powerful tightening lessened and came to a rest, and Holly realized what Blaire had meant when she had written about being transported into another world. With that last pain, Holly herself had felt she was lifted out of this world, so deeply consumed by the intensity of it that there was nothing else to consider other than making it through the powerful wave.

Returning to Earth, Holly exhaled deeply. She knew she didn't have very much time before the next one, so she staggered into the dimly lit bedroom and pulled herself up onto the bed. As she slid to the center of the bed and propped herself on her knees and elbows, she silently wondered again how much longer she would have to endure the pain. She desperately hoped that it wouldn't be much longer. Surely it *couldn't* be much longer, she briefly thought.

As the next wave quickly approached, there was an immense force of pressure in Holly's bottom. She was unable to control her body's impulse to bear down; it was inescapable, her body seeming to know just what to do.

A gush of water let loose, and what seemed like a gallon of clear liquid poured onto the bed beneath Holly. In that same moment, she experienced the painful burning sensation that Blaire had described. Her bottom did indeed burn with the intensity of a fiery branding iron. She felt the hard, round protrusion that was the baby's head emerging from within her.

Holly swiftly pulled herself up to the head of the bed and held onto the headboard with both hands as she propped herself on her knees. Her tender skin stretched to allow the baby's crown to protrude, and she felt sure that her skin was tearing. The next squeeze came quickly and brought the baby's entire head out. She cradled the baby's wet face in her hands as her body continued to work. Adrenaline permeated her blood with each beat of her quivering heart.

One more surge from within her body swiftly pushed the rest of the baby out. Shocked, Holly brought the gray-tinged baby to her chest. The baby was so slippery that she was careful not to allow it to slip through her hands. As she lowered the tiny newborn back down in front of her to admire and rub, a small, cough-like sound was followed by the tiniest, most precious wail that Holly had ever heard.

She rocked and shushed and rubbed the wet, slick babe as its skin began to turn pink before her teary eyes. She continued holding the baby close as she soared into a high place that she had never entered before.

Checking between the baby's chubby legs, she realized that she was meeting her daughter for the first time.

"How can I love you this much already?" she cooed through sobs.

Holly reached down to the foot of the bed and grabbed the small yellow blanket she had laid out only an hour before. She wrapped the baby in it, loosely, then pulled her up to her in the crook of her arm.

The white, limp umbilical cord still tied the two together, and Holly wasn't sure how long it would take for her to deliver the afterbirth. That was something Blaire hadn't mentioned in her diary, but she assumed it wouldn't be very long.

The baby quieted and met Holly's gaze as she

rocked her and stroked her tiny pink cheek. Wet swirls of light brown hair clung to her perfectly round head. Holly was so thankful for the cottage that she was able to give birth in. She couldn't imagine if she had gone into labor out in the street somewhere, or even in an empty restaurant. Everything she needed was here…shelter, warmth, food, and her perfect baby girl.

The two of them looked into each other's eyes for a long while–Holly wasn't sure how long it had been; she had completely lost track of time as she soared high above the stars. Her focus was interrupted when the placenta detached and was expelled onto the bed between her blood-streaked legs.

"I am in a total mess," she said through laughter before fixing her gaze on the baby again.

As if in response to her statement, the baby's mouth turned up in the slightest, sweetest smile Holly had ever seen. Tears seemed to be in a continuous flow from her eyes as she admired every tiny feature. Her heart pounded with euphoria.

Reaching over as far as she could, Holly grasped the strap of her bag from its place on the dresser. She unzipped the front pocket with her left hand and felt inside it until her fingers landed on what she needed.

Careful not to go near the baby with it, she opened her pocket knife with the brisk flick of her wrist. Then, grasping the slender, cold umbilical cord with her right hand, she quickly and carefully severed the cord before folding the knife and slipping it back into its place.

"You're going to have to have a name, aren't you?" Holly cooed toward the baby as she rewrapped her in the soft, yellow blanket.

She had had a name in mind for a baby girl all along. She wanted to name the baby–whether boy or girl- after Grandpa. She would go with Ivy, she decided. After the greatest man she had ever known: Cecil Ivy.

"I think Ivy suits you beautifully," she said before kissing baby Ivy's petal-soft forehead.

Again, Ivy responded to her mother's voice…this time with a whimper.

"Oh, s-h-h-h-h," Holly whispered.

"Are you ready to nurse?"

As soon as the words left her lips, the baby began turning her little head back and forth against Holly's bare chest, her tiny pink mouth opened in a perfect *O* shape.

Holly began an attempt to nurse Ivy. She had no experience whatsoever in nursing a baby and, of course, had no one there to teach her. However, she found that she needed neither one, as the baby latched on and began suckling instinctively and effortlessly. Holly smiled with satisfaction and gratefulness as she watched her nursing baby girl in awe.

With her index finger wrapped in baby Ivy's tiny, wrinkled fingers, Holly could feel the adrenaline dissipating from her body, and she realized she was quite tired. In the stillness of the quiet cottage by the sea, she succumbed to the weight of her exhaustion and drifted softly to sleep.

SEVEN

Holly had awoken to the smell of the soup simmering on the stove, disoriented about the time of day. She was glad she had added the water to it, but it was still a wonder that the soup had not boiled dry and burned. She had no idea how long it had been warming. She had no idea what time she had given birth, only that it was in the afternoon. She thought it was still daylight when the baby was born, though she couldn't be entirely sure because the curtains were drawn and only the very small lamp on the nightstand lit the bedroom.

Baby Ivy slept peacefully on the seemingly gigantic bed while Holly feebly cleaned up the mess. She had managed to get the bloody linens into the washing machine and started the wash cycle, moving extra slowly as she did so. She chopped up the placenta and flushed it down the toilet, bit by bit. Then she took the oldest-looking wash cloths she could find to use in her underwear as well as for the baby's bottom, since she had no disposable diapers or feminine pads.

Once everything was cleaned up, Holly leaned

over the bed and studied the sleeping baby closely. She kissed her tiny hand and left the room for the kitchen. There, she made a fresh cup of the *'wellness tea'* that she'd found in the cupboard and prepared herself a steamy bowl of the chicken noodle soup. She took both the soup and tea back into the bedroom with her and carefully set them on the nightstand before climbing into bed next to sleeping baby Ivy.

The mug and bowl on the nightstand both steamed and smelled very pleasing. As they cooled, Holly reached for Blaire's diary. She could use a little encouragement while her supper cooled. Carefully scooting the tiny little bundle up next to her crossed legs, she opened the diary to the page where she'd left off.

EIGHT

Today has been very peaceful and relaxing. *Violet and I went down to the beach early this morning and scanned the shore for shells and seaglass. We each came back with pockets full of sand and seashells. I perked some coffee while Violet whipped up some peach pancakes and we enjoyed breakfast on the back porch in the salty morning breeze.*

After we cleaned up the breakfast dishes, we decided to visit our two favorite antique shops. Both have great prices and, as a bonus, live-in cats that prance around and rub against our legs, so of course they have to be the best! We sauntered around every square foot of each store, browsing each section slowly. I found a handmade quilt in perfect condition and some pretty brass candle holders. Violet bought some wall art and some goat's milk soap.

Afterward, we stopped at Cora's Deli for lunch before heading back to the cottage. The rest of the day was spent lying on the beach, soaking up the glorious sun. I nearly fell asleep while listening to the sounds of the waves and the seagulls, the breeze licking my tanned skin.

I couldn't help but think, as Violet and I went about our leisurely day, how much things change over the course of one's life. For so many years, I was fully immersed in all of the wonderful, demanding duties of being a homemaker and mother of four. The saying goes..."The days are long, but the years are short..." That is so very true. Some days felt like they'd never end. Sick days and emotionally charged days and everything in between, all the while keeping everyone fed, happy, and clean.

I could never have imagined a day like today, where nobody would depend on me to tell them where their hat was, or pour their milk, or change their diaper. I know Violet feels the same way; we were just talking about it earlier today. Yet here we both are, in a slower season of life.

There was a time when walking through an antique store meant keeping both eyes on all the children, a hand on Aaron at all times lest he'd run off or climb on something fragile, and being prepared to pay for something broken.

But as I think back on those days that are long gone, I find that I miss them. I don't miss meltdowns and tantrums, or spills, or fights. But I do so miss little hands that were small enough to fit in my palm, and bedtime stories, and ten thousand questions per hour. I miss dirty faces and smiles of pride as they brought me a flower they'd picked from my special flower garden.

Though my childrens' younger years were all very special in every phase, I must be partial to those magical first few weeks of their lives.

I remember everything being so fresh and uncertain when Sarah was born. It felt almost as if I was the only one to ever have a newborn to care for, as silly as it sounds! Still, though, I seemed to intuitively know what to do to care for her. Of course, I did have Violet to guide me and to reassure me, given that she had had several children to my one.

I think all mothers —even first-time mothers— know what to do, truly. They may seem afraid, as I did. But we all have the innate instinct deep inside of us that we can lean into if we dare to. It's comforting to get the opinions of those more experienced, but ultimately, I feel that we always know what is best for our own babies.

As I looked down at tiny baby Sarah almost constantly, I just couldn't believe she was actually mine. That was my first thought....she couldn't possibly be mine because she was just too beautiful to have come from me.

As I watched the little faces she made in her sleep, I wondered who she would grow up to be. I cried as I vowed to myself and to her that I would love her with every ounce of my being, for as long as I lived. Each whimper was attended to diligently, and that never changed for any of my babies. I never believed for a second that a tiny newborn should cry itself to sleep, or that it knew how to manipulate me. When they had a need, I was there to help them. And I still feel that way today. Though my girls have husbands now and don't rely on me any longer, I will always try to help them should they ever need me...that much will never change.

I remember counting Sarah's wet diapers, trying to make sure she had enough per day. If she didn't wet her diaper for several hours, I would worry. If she slept through a nursing session, I would worry. I woke several times during the night to make sure she was breathing. I worried that she wasn't crawling soon enough, then that she wasn't walking soon enough. Even with Violet's assurance that everything would be fine, I still seemed to worry about little Sarah. It felt like every little thing she did was specific to only her — no other baby had ever done these things before, in the history of mankind! It is funny to think back on, now. Everything <u>was </u>fine, indeed. There was no need to trouble my mind about Sarah's milestones or anything else. I realize now, after having three more babies after her, that I would have known without a doubt if something had truly been wrong.

Once, I took Sarah to the doctor because she wouldn't stop spitting up. Every time she nursed, she threw the milk right back up. I thought that surely she could not be keeping enough down to sustain her, so I expressed my concern to the doctor. He assured me that until the baby's internal organs shifted and spread out into their proper place, her stomach would be a bit squished in there. He said her small stomach would only hold about a teaspoon at a time – I didn't need to worry. But still, I argued with him that she threw up way too much. He couldn't possibly know just how much; he wasn't with her twenty-four seven like I was. It was enough to soil the entire front of her little gowns, and it was after every single feeding.

At my apparent distress and need for some sort of validation or solution, the doctor said he would prescribe a liquid antacid for her. That satisfied me, which was the main purpose of his intervention, I am most certain.

I went straight to the drug store and picked up the antacid, and once home, I placed the bottle in the medicine cabinet, where it stayed unopened until I finally threw it away years later.

Violet had tried to tell me that all of her babies threw up a lot, but I just didn't believe they could have <u>possibly</u> thrown up as much as Sarah. No, she was definitely a special case. Something was the matter with her, I feared.

Yet, I never cracked open that bottle of medicine. Though I didn't feel quite right about giving it to her, I think I just needed to 'do something' about the supposed issue. I don't know…maybe there were still remnants of my nursing indoctrination that needed to wear off. But later that year, when that very same antacid was deemed unsafe and recalled, I was so very thankful that I never gave any of it to my Sarah.

Once Maeve, Addie, and then Aaron came along, I began to believe what my sister Violet had said when Sarah was just a tiny baby..."Most things will be better in the morning. Don't fret!" She was indeed right, that most things did resolve on their own, and with no help from any fretting. When I learned to trust my intuition, motherhood became first-nature, as it should have been from the start.

Often, I reflect on my days of mothering small children. It proves to be bittersweet, but mostly sweet...I have the precious memories to reflect on, wonderful adult children as the product of the nurturing Joseph and I took so seriously...and Violet and I get to vacation and dilly-dally as much as we want to as I eagerly await grandchildren.

Oh, I just can't wait to see the face of my first grand-baby. I can't wait to hold and to smell them, and to be reminded of the days when I held their mother – or father, but I am assuming one of my already-married girls will have a baby before Aaron becomes a father. He hasn't even found a wife yet!

I can hardly wait to bring the grandchildren here with me...to build sandcastles with and buy limitless snowcones for. We will play in the sand all day long, dine on sandwiches in the breeze under the shade of the palmetto trees, and sleep deeply at night to the sound of the ocean, while cuddled up in bed together.

Well...I suppose that's enough reflection for one day. It has been nice and restorative. I think Violet and I will probably end the day with a steak dinner on the porch and a peaceful evening walk along the shore. Violet just talked to John on the phone and is now beginning to prepare the salad greens. Maybe she and I will walk to the coffee shop down the street for an iced latte, later. It will be a nice, refreshing treat in the balminess of the salty, summer air.

Until next time,
Blaire

NINE

Just as Holly was closing the diary, she heard a sound. Baby Ivy seemed to hear it too, as she startled momentarily, tossing up her tiny hands, but then went on sleeping. 'Here we go,' thought Holly. She scooped Ivy up and took a few deep breaths as she held her to her chest.

She wasn't afraid; she knew this moment would come, eventually. She just didn't know when. It was better for it to happen now, though. She needed it, after all.

The sound of the deadbolt unlocking was followed by the creaking of the front door. She had left the light on underneath the stove's hood vent, and the soup and cookies were still out. They would realize someone was here before they entered the bedroom and found her and baby Ivy.

'Could it be Blaire?' she wondered as she sat in bed, tensed up. If it were Blaire or Violet, Holly knew they would be kind and understanding. She closed her eyes and imagined the footsteps she heard coming across the kitchen floor to be Blaire's.

But they didn't belong to Blaire or Violet. Instead, Holly opened her eyes to see a young man standing in the doorway of the bedroom. He looked startled as he took a step back.

"Whoa," he said, raising his hands up in front of him.

"I don't mean to scare you, Miss."

His strawberry blonde hair was neatly swooped across his forehead, and even in the dim light, Holly could tell his eyes were as blue as the ocean. He wore a denim jacket over a plaid flannel shirt, reminding her of Grandpa.

Holly didn't quite know what to say to the young man. At first, she just stared at him as she clung tightly to baby Ivy.

"Who are you?" she finally asked, in more of a cheerful tone so as not to offend him. He didn't seem to be a threat to her, after all.

"My name is Aaron…" he answered as if he were asking a question.

"This is my Aunt's house, and my mother sent me here to get something… Are you okay?" he asked, clearly concerned.

Holly felt the tension melting away.

"We're doing fine," she answered with a smile as she looked down at the sleeping Ivy and kissed her forehead.

"What's today's date?" Holly asked.

"It's December 20th," a puzzled Aaron answered, brows furrowed.

December 20th. What a great day to be born, she thought as she rubbed the blanket that covered Ivy's back.

"Happy belated Birthday, then," she said, surprising Aaron.

He chuckled nervously.

"Do I know you?" he asked, curiously.

"No," Holly answered. "But I know a little bit about *you.*"

Aaron looked increasingly puzzled, but he kept his distance in the doorway. Holly appreciated that.

He scratched his head and then leaned against the door jamb.

"You do, do you?" Aaron asked.

"I do…" Holly picked up the diary from the bed and held it up.

"I've been reading your mother's diary," she admitted.

Aaron was still dumbfounded, but he snickered as he pulled a toothpick from behind his ear.

"Well, who are you?" he asked, looking at Holly rather sheepishly.

"My name's Holly," she answered, knowing that it didn't really answer his question.

"You can come in," she said, pointing toward the winged back chair in the corner. "I'm all right right here," he replied with a nod.

"Suit yourself," Holly said before continuing. "I've been sort of *squatting* here, I guess."

She looked down at the bed. Saying the words aloud brought with them an embarrassing sort of sting.

"Well, are you *all right,* though…" Aaron seemed to make more of a statement than to ask a question. He continued to wear an expression of deep concern as he chewed on the toothpick.

"I'm all right," Holly replied. "We have nowhere to go, though."

As she said it, a tear slipped down her cheek. Today was only the second time she had allowed herself to cry since running away from home. The first time, of course, was in the moments after Ivy was born.

As Aaron gazed from Holly to Ivy and back again, his look of concern turned to one of genuine sadness.

"Well," he stopped.

"You don't have to worry about that. You can stay here as long as you need to."

"Do you mind me asking your story, though? I mean, where do you come from?" Aaron questioned.

Holly sat silently for a moment.

"I ran away," she finally answered as another tear streaked her face.

Aaron nodded but said nothing.

"I ran away from her father," she said, glancing down at baby Ivy.

"He is awfully mean," she continued. "My grandpa was the only protection I had from Colt… and he passed away."

She continued, "I am from the mountains of Tennessee. My home has always been there…always will be there. But I just had to get away for the baby's sake."

"How did you get *here*?" Aaron asked.

"Uh – Well, I snuck off to the bus stop late at night, and the bus brought me here," she answered matter-of-factly as she dabbed the tears from her face.

"I sure have been grateful to have found this house, too," Holly continued.

"When did you have the baby?" Aaron asked, nodding toward little Ivy.

"Just today," she replied, thinking that the day had been impossibly long.

"I'm not sure what time it was–"

"I'd better call my Mama, I think," Aaron said, feeling each of his pockets as he looked for his phone.

"Blaire?" Holly asked with a smile, already knowing the answer.

"Mm hmm," Aaron answered with a faint smile, as he brought the phone to his ear.

He walked into the kitchen, and Holly sat perfectly still and quiet, listening as he softly spoke with Blaire.

"I think so," she heard him whisper through the phone.

"Yes, ma'am. I'll ask her…"

"All right. Yes, ma'am. Okay. Love you. Bye."

Aaron reappeared in the bedroom's doorway.

"Have you eaten or drank anything since the baby was born?" he asked.

"I'm working on this soup and tea," Holly answered, nodding toward the nightstand.

"And—" he began. "I hate to ask you this…but you're not losing a whole lot of blood, are you?"

Holly could tell Aaron didn't want to ask about such things as he squirmed and cracked his knuckles.

She shrugged. "I don't think so. And I mean, I don't feel faint or anything like that."

"Okay." Aaron nodded, seemingly satisfied with her answer.

"Now…" He finally entered the room and perched his leg on the chest by the foot of the bed.

"Would you come home with me?"

Holly didn't know what to say. The question took her by surprise, and she felt her heart pick up the pace.

"Where is home?" she asked curiously. She already knew she would go with him, no matter what the answer was. She didn't have very much choice in the matter, unless she was given permission to stay in the beach cottage. And actually, he had already told her she could stay there, hadn't he?

"Weatherford, North Carolina," he replied. "About two hours North of here."

She mulled it over in her mind, though most of it was a facade.

"Well…I guess so," Holly answered.

"You're up for it…you're sure?" he asked.

"I don't see why not," she shrugged.

"Okay, then. Let's get you ready."

Aaron slapped his thigh as he stood straight and glanced around the room.

"I don't have much to pack, at least," Holly said.

"I'll help you; you just tell me what you need," Aaron said as he looked around for things to gather.

"Well, there are some wet linens still in the washing machine…" Holly began.

"That's okay. I'll grab a trash bag to put them in, and we will dry them when we get home."

Aaron headed straight for the kitchen and returned momentarily with the trash bag in hand. He went down the little hallway to the dryer, where he pulled the clean, wet linens out and placed them carefully in the bag.

Holly watched him from the bed. She noted how he didn't toss, sling, or jerk things, even when he was in a hurry. He was calm, gentle, and kind. Just the way Blaire had described him.

Holly hoped the bloody linens had come clean in the washing machine, mainly because he didn't want Aaron to be disgusted or embarrassed by them. From what she could tell from the bed, things appeared clean as he dropped them into the open trash bag.

Holly unwrapped sleeping baby Ivy and checked the rag to see if she needed a change. She gently wiped the baby's bottom with a wet cloth and placed a clean washcloth between her legs, fanning it out in front and across her bottom. Then, she wrapped her snugly in the soft, warm blanket again and held her close, Ivy never even waking up.

Aaron checked the dryer before turning and heading back down the hallway toward the bedroom. He pointed to the restroom as he passed by it.

"Do you need me to pack anything in here?" he asked.

"It's okay," Holly answered. "I can do it."

"You should rest," he gently argued. "I will do everything that needs doing."

"That's so kind of you. But I will be okay. I just need to go use the restroom and grab my things out of there. You can start putting things away I've left out in the kitchen, if you want to." Holly hoped Aaron wouldn't argue further, or else she would just have to embarrass him by telling him frankly that she needed to get up so she could change her underwear.

He didn't object. Instead, he nodded and headed through the doorway and into the kitchen. She could hear silverware clinging and pots banging as he put away the clean dishes she had washed and left on a dish towel to dry. There had been a dishwasher, but Holly didn't know how to use one anyway, so she had hand-washed every dish she had used.

Leaving Ivy sleeping peacefully on the bed, Holly slipped quickly and quietly down the short hallway and into the restroom. She scanned the small room for anything she had brought with her, seeing nothing but her toothbrush. She quickly packed it in her bag, then she cleaned herself up and tied up the bathroom trash bag, taking it and her backpack with her as she turned out the light and left the room.

None of her personal belongings were in the bedroom – except her baby, of course. She checked on Ivy and grabbed the soup bowl and tea cup off the nightstand as she passed through to the kitchen, where Aaron was busy putting the soup remnants in the refrigerator. She cleared her throat as she drew a little nearer to him. Aaron turned toward her quickly, smiling as soon as he saw her.

"I tried not to make too big a mess," she said, taking the dishes to the sink and rinsing them out. "I'll clean those," Aaron said, walking toward the sink.

Holly chuckled. "Okay, okay." She backed away, holding both hands up.

"Hey, what did you come all the way here to get, anyway?" Holly prodded.

"Shoot. I sure am glad you said that, or else I might have left here without it. Wouldn't that be something?" he snickered. Then he continued, "Of all things, Mama sent me down here to get a punch bowl."

Holly laughed, taking a step back to peek in the doorway of the bedroom. Ivy was still sleeping peacefully on the bed by the light of the glowing lamp.

"*A punch bowl?*" Holly asked.

"That's right. It seems she left it here sometime over the summer. I don't know, I think she and Aunt

Violet and some more ladies had a party here, and she had brought her Christmas punch bowl down for it. And now she needs it…nothing will do but for her to have that punch bowl on Christmas." Aaron laughed, shaking his head.

"I would do anything for her, though, I reckon," he added, placing the clean dishes on the towel after he'd rinsed them.

"That's sweet," Holly commented. "Do you know where to find it?"

"It's supposed to be in this cabinet right….here," he said, moving to the large cherrywood hutch straight ahead. Kneeling, he opened both doors at the bottom of the hutch.

"And here it is," he said, pulling a large brass basin from the dark cabinet. Ladle's here too," he grunted as he stood, holding the punch bowl in both of his large hands.

"That's pretty," Holly commented. "Is your mom having a big gathering for Christmas?"

"It'll just be the family. Me, my daddy, my sisters, their husbands, Aunt Violet, Uncle John, and the cousins. Plus, I think Mama has invited the man who delivers mail." Aaron snickered. "It seems we always have one or two extra around the table. And it looks like we'll have you and the baby this year, too."

"Is it a girl or a boy?" he asked, seemingly regretful that he had not shown interest in the baby before.

"It's a girl," Holly answered proudly. "Ivy is her name. After my Grandpa Ivy."

"Holly and Ivy. Well, I'll be. That's just fitting for Christmas time, ain't it?"

Aaron had a sort of boyish innocence about him, but it was overshadowed by the masculinity that dominated his existence.

"I guess it is, since you mentioned it," Holly agreed with a polite smile.

"Well, I guess we're about ready to go, once you get everything you need," Aaron said, carrying the punch bowl toward the living room.

Holly stood alone in the kitchen for just a moment. She was thankful for this cottage and for everything the small, abundant kitchen provided for her when she most needed it.

She turned and went into the bedroom, where she carefully gathered the baby and held her to her chest as she turned the lamp off and dragged her backpack across the floor.

"I'll get that," Aaron insisted, pointing at the bag when she emerged from the bedroom.

She let go of the strap and adjusted Ivy in her arms.

"Thank you," she said, as he approached them and scooped up the bag, making it look as light as a feather.

"Yes, ma'am. Is this everything?" he asked, looking from the bag to Holly.

"That's it."

As the three of them left the small beachfront

cottage and faced the cool, dark night, Holly felt safer than she had at any time since meeting Colt. Even safer than when she was at home with Grandpa, and that was hard to top.

The houses all down the street had colorful Christmas lights hanging from the eaves of their homes. Trees glistened in the windows, and the palmetto tree trunks in some of the yards were wrapped in thousands of brightly glowing lights.

"Do you have enough clothes on?" Aaron asked as they carefully inched down the porch steps. "Mama said for me not to let you get cold. And the baby…do you think she's warm enough?"

"We're fine. We're just fine," Holly assured him. "You have heat in the car, right?"

"In this one, yes. It's Mama's car." He chuckled as he opened the passenger door for her.

"I guess you'll have to just hold her while we drive. But I'll stop at the nearest Walmart and buy her a car seat, and whatever else you need –"

Holly reached out and lightly grasped his forearm.

"Thank you," she said, before taking a seat in the car's slick leather seat.

As they pulled away from the cottage and headed down the street toward the highway, Holly noticed the care that Aaron took as he drove them. Checking his mirrors often, he drove with both hands on the wheel, staying just below the speed limit. She exhaled long and slow with feelings of gratitude and relief as she pressed her lips to baby Ivy's warm, soft forehead.

It was quiet for a while as they drove in the night. The smell of leather penetrated Holly's senses, making for a future fragrance flashback, the way the smell of cigar smoke took her back to the old days when Uncle Henry would visit Grandpa and her. The men would sit outside on the front porch in the rocking chairs while Holly swung back and forth on the creaky porch swing. Uncle Henry always brought an orange for her. He would take the orange in one hand, reach into his overall pocket for his knife, and then carve a small hole in the orange with the sharp pocketknife before bending down and handing it to Holly, all the while a long, brown cigar sticking out of his mouth. She squealed with delight as she took the orange and ran to the swing to begin sucking the juice out of it.

The stretch of highway before Holly was mostly bare, with only a few other cars dotting it. She was glad of that; it meant there was less chance they would have an accident with baby Ivy.

Aaron's voice broke the silence. "It's only a couple of miles to the exit where the store is. When we get there, I want you to write down anything at all that you or the baby needs. Or want, for that matter."

Holly began to feel emotional as the stranger offered to take care of her and her baby. It's not as if he were obligated to do anything for them.

"I really hate for you to do that, Aaron. I have no way at all to pay you back. You know that, don't you?"

She hoped he wouldn't say something absurd, insinuating that she could pay him back in other ways.

"I'm not asking you to pay me back," he replied instead. "This isn't going to be a loan; it's just going to be a gift."

Holly's throat clenched, and she made an unsuccessful attempt to swallow before responding to him. Her eyes stung as she finally spoke.

"I know it's not enough, but thank you."

Aaron didn't say anything, but in the light of the town's street lamps, he glanced over at her. She thought she saw a trickle of a smile as he turned back toward the road. They pulled into Walmart, and Holly noticed the parking lot was more than half full. She looked at the clock above the car's radio. It read 6:26 p.m. It felt much later.

As they pulled into a parking spot, Aaron sifted through the console before pulling out a scrap of paper and an ink pen.

"Okay, do you want me to write? I know you've got your hands full."

"Sure...you can," Holly replied sheepishly. "Um...well, some diapers would be really nice." She chuckled lightly.

Aaron wrote down diapers, wipes, newborn pajamas, and some feminine products for Holly before adding his own items below them.

"She needs a safe car seat," he said, nodding toward Ivy, who was still sleeping soundly in Holly's arms.

Holly just looked at Aaron with a combination of surrender and gratitude in her eyes.

Aaron met her eyes but then looked back at the list in his hand. He seemed to have quite the list going, but she didn't spy.

As he opened the door, the cold wind swept in, sending a chill down Holly's spine. She was careful not to shiver and cause Aaron to feel guilty. "I'm locking you in and leaving the car running. I'll be back as soon as I can, I promise."

Then, he shut the car door and was off across the parking lot, leaving Holly and Ivy safe and warm in the car. Everything was unfamiliar to her. The car, the town, Aaron, even Ivy. Yet she felt comfortable beyond her own understanding.

As she looked around the parking lot at the light posts wrapped in white Christmas lights, she felt peaceful enough that she could have fallen asleep. The passersby kept her awake and vigilant, and a few even provided a bit of comedy for her, including the man who hit his shin on his own trailer hitch and cursed aloud before looking around to see if anyone saw him. Holly escaped unseen.

She decided to try to nurse Ivy while they waited. She was afraid she would wake up hungry during the remainder of the trip. As she brought the baby to her breast, Ivy slowly turned her head back and forth in search of the nipple before latching. Holly winced slightly as she latched and suckled. She was sure the tenderness would fade, but even if it didn't, it was all right.

Soon, Holly saw Aaron walking toward the car, pushing a shopping buggy that appeared to be filled to the brim. "What in the world has he bought?" she wondered aloud.

She unlocked the door as he approached the car. She could see the large box that contained the car seat, which took up the majority of the space in the buggy.

Aaron opened the back door and started stuffing bags in. "Which side do you want the car seat on? Do you want to ride back here with her?"

Holly turned to face him. "Um—-It doesn't matter which side. I'll probably ride back there with her if that's okay."

"More than okay. Whatever you want," Aaron replied as he piled more bags onto the floorboard.

"Do you need to go inside and use the restroom or anything? I got these…" he carefully laid a grocery bag on the console next to Holly, and she could see through the bag that there was a package of *Depends* inside. He continued to be busy at work with the rest of the bags.

"I know you don't want to leave the baby out here. I can come into the store with you and hold her for you or something. You can even keep my keys, and I don't have a spare."

Holly smiled at his thoughtfulness. "You're too kind… I think I'm okay for now, though. I'll just lay

Ivy down in the back seat and get her changed."

"All right. I'll take the buggy back and then get this car seat installed back here," Aaron said as he placed the last of the bags on the leather seat.

Holly pulled the blanket up over the back of the baby's tiny head before opening the passenger door and moving to the back seat of the car. The wind was strong and cold, blowing her long hair against her face.

Once in the back, she closed the door and lay Ivy down on the soft seat. Holly sifted carefully through the plastic bags until she found the diapers and baby wipes. As she fastened one of them onto baby Ivy's tiny bottom, she thought having the disposable diaper felt like a luxury, and one that she was thankful to have.

Next, she found a tiny, soft pink onesie. She held it up and admired its tiny size. 'How could anyone fit into an outfit so small?' she asked herself as she looked down at the one who would indeed fit perfectly into it.

Ivy slept through both her diaper change and being clothed for the very first time. She looked so sweet in her soft little outfit that Holly could hardly stand it. She picked her up off the car seat and held her close, kissing her soft, milky-smelling cheeks.

"Oh, you smell so *good*," she cooed.

Aaron was painstakingly reading the instruction manual for how to install the car seat while she dressed baby Ivy. He sat across from them on the seat with the door open, using the car's interior light to read by.

"There are a lot of rules," he commented as he held

the manual up.

Holly chuckled. "I'm sorry. Is it going to be a pain to put in?"

"Oh, no. I've got it. I just want to make sure I'm doing it exactly right. I mean, I know we just rode with her up front without a car seat at all, but now that we've got one, it's got to be right. We're still a good way from home yet."

Holly smiled as she exhaled slowly against Ivy's soft, golden brown hair.

As Aaron carefully read and worked to get the seat in place just so, Holly had a snack from the bag he'd given her and told her to eat from it. He had gotten her an assortment of fruit and nuts, raisin bread, and a bottle of eggnog.

"I don't even know if you like that stuff," he said bashfully. "But if you don't, I also have some orange juice and water in here; you just take your pick."

"I actually *do* like eggnog," Holly admitted with a snicker. "I always have. Thank you."

Holly knew the spicy taste of the eggnog would confirm that it was indeed Christmastime. So far, she had been having a hard time believing it. Aside from the greatest gift she had ever received, it hadn't felt much like Christmas to her. Grandpa always bought a carton of eggnog for Holly and himself every year just before Christmas.

"Even the store-bought kind? I'm sure it's not like homemade eggnog, but I thought it might be a welcome treat."

"Oh, store-bought is all I know." Holly laughed.

"Then, you're in for a treat when we get home. I imagine Mama is home cooking up a storm right now, getting everything ready for Christmas Eve…and that punch bowl back there in the truck she sent me after has a special purpose."

"Eggnog?" Holly guessed.

"Yep. Every year," Aaron answered.

"Well, I sure am glad she forgot her punch bowl at the beach house, I can tell you that much. How unlikely is that, anyway? Her Christmas punch bowl was left all the way down here, and she didn't even realize it until five days before Christmas."

"I know, it is funny how it happened. Lucky, too," he said, glancing over his shoulder at Holly as they sailed down the highway toward Weatherford.

Little Ivy continued to sleep peacefully with Holly keeping a close eye on her, feeling for the warmth of her breath often.

'Home,' Aaron had said. She had liked the way he'd said it. 'When we get home.' Holly was beginning to believe she and Ivy might be out of Colt's reach for sure.

92

TEN

Holly and Aaron hadn't talked about much by way of personal topics on the drive to Weatherford. They'd made cordial small talk, but nothing beyond that. She was thankful that he hadn't pried, although it wasn't so much that she minded telling him whatever it was he might want to know. It was more about the fact that he had a proper gauge for knowing when and what to say to a woman who had given birth only hours before. Aaron seemed to be sensitive and respectful, and though she wouldn't let him know it, she already trusted him completely.

"We're almost there. Are you still awake back there?" Aaron asked in a hushed tone as they drove down the winding country road.

"Yeah, I am. Just thinking about how these curvy backroads remind me of home in Tennessee," she answered. "I'll bet everything is covered with snow up there, though."

"There's nothing like a white Christmas. We don't

get too many of those down here. I can only remember maybe two Christmases in my life where we had snow on the ground."

"Oh, no… that's kind of sad!"

In contrast, Holly remembered only a couple of Christmases in her lifetime when there *wasn't* snow on the ground.

"But don't worry. We do get plenty of snow; it just hasn't happened close to Christmas very many times. It gets plenty cold, though. I know Mama and Daddy have the woodstove doing all it can do at home right now." Aaron chuckled.

Now that she could put a face to the stories Blaire had written in her diary, Holly imagined Aaron chopping firewood and hauling it into the house for the family. His big hands were probably calloused and splinter-resistant.

"Oh, I'm not really sad about it," Holly replied. "To be honest, my favorite thing about home wasn't even the snow… It was fall. Grandpa and I both loved to go for drives in his old Ford pickup every year as the leaves began to change and turn loose, before the first snow of the year. We would ride along slowly while listening to the local radio station. You could smell the wood smoke from the houses we passed, and see the trail of smoke puffing out of the chimneys. I felt so content in that truck with Grandpa."

Holly grew silent for a moment. Then she spoke up again.

"I'm sorry; I don't know why I told you that." She laughed nervously.

"It's all right," Aaron said. "It sounds like it meant a lot to you. Besides, I like hearing about other folks' experiences."

There was silence and darkness between them for a few long moments. Baby Ivy whimpered ever so slightly in her sleep.

"Well, here we are, up ahead. And I hope you're ready to meet my family, because I have no doubt they are chomping at the bit to meet you and the baby."

"Really?" Holly asked.

"Oh, yeah. I'm sure of it. Mama is crazy about babies, and she and Daddy both love company."

"That makes me a little nervous." Holly giggled.

"You've got nothing to be nervous about," Aaron assured her. "They're friendly people, and they're going to take right up with the both of you."

"I feel like I know Blaire – uh, your mama, already." Suddenly, Holly gasped.

"Oh, do you think she will be upset with me for reading her personal diary?" she asked, worriedly. "I never in a million years thought I'd meet the person who wrote it. I never thought she would even know that anyone had read it, at all."

"She won't mind," he said. "Did she ever mention anyone by the name of Old Addie in her diary?"

"Yes, actually. She did."

"Well, I don't know if she mentioned this or not,

but she started snooping in the first of Old Addie's diaries long before she knew who she was. The only difference is that Old Addie is dead, so she can't even be mad at her." Aaron chuckled as he turned the car into the driveway.

"I'm not sure if that makes me feel better or not," Holly replied with a snicker. "I suppose it does, though. Maybe she will forgive me."

"I'm sure of it."

The house was aglow with glistening yellow lights twisted around the porch posts. The full, multi-colored Christmas tree stood in the front-facing window. It appeared that every light in the house was on. A trail of smoke billowed from the chimney, and Holly smelled the nostalgic scent of the burning wood in the air as Aaron opened the car door for her.

He stepped aside and waited as Holly carefully stood from the car, cradling baby Ivy in her arms. The wind swirled around them, raising chill bumps on Holly's skin as she wrapped Ivy tighter in the blanket and held her to her chest.

"I'll come back for those bags. Let's just get you two in the house where it's warm."

Aaron walked alongside them as they took the walkway and approached the towering white farmhouse. Her breath made white puffs of smoke in the night air.

Holly felt both nervous excitement and an odd peace as she climbed the two porch steps and faced the front door of Blaire's house. Aaron went ahead of her and opened the creaky door, stepping aside to make room for her to step in.

Inside, she was immediately blanketed with a heavy, comforting warmth that seemed to penetrate the deepest parts of her bones. The house smelled of baking ham combined with coffee and cinnamon.

Her gaze immediately flashed to the woman of the house. Wearing a broad, sincere smile and all of her blonde-gray hair pulled back, Blaire quickly approached Holly and baby Ivy. She wasn't quite how Holly had envisioned her, but she was even more beautiful. She wore a dark green apron, spotted with flour and cocoa. As she came closer, Holly noticed the small wrinkles around her light blue eyes. Her cheeks were rosy and uplifted as she grinned, revealing porcelain-white teeth that were imperfect but beautiful.

Blaire took Holly by her shoulders with both hands before sliding one of them down to caress baby Ivy's back.

"How wonderful to have you!" she beamed.

"Thank you very much," Holly said. She couldn't deny that she felt a bit self-conscious. Maybe the raw vulnerability that came with just having birthed your first child was partially to blame, but Holly somehow felt ashamed that she wasn't as wise or seasoned with age in the way that Blaire was.

"Come, please have a seat," Blaire said, motioning toward the large sofa in the middle of the living room.

"This is Joseph," she said, pointing to him as he sat in his easy chair, cracking pecans.

At his introduction, he smiled and nodded. "How are you?" he said, though it sounded more like a statement than a question. But he was polite; Holly could tell.

As she took a seat on the soft couch, Blaire sat down next to her.

"Well, how *are* you, honey?" she asked.

"I'm doing pretty good, I think," Holly replied, laying Ivy down in the crook of her arm.

"Look at that precious thing. And born just today; I can hardly believe it," Blaire beamed.

"I still can't believe it, myself. I think this has been the longest day I've ever had."

"I know you must be worn out. Are you?"

"I am starting to feel it again. The adrenaline kicks in every now and then, but I think I can sleep tonight," Holly snickered.

"Do you want me to show you where you'll sleep?" Blaire asked. "Then we'll have supper. I have a beef roast with mashed potatoes and all the fixins – Oh, Aaron. You *didn't* forget my punch bowl… did you?"

"No ma'am. It's in the car. I'll go out and get it along with the other things." He looked at Holly as he said it, getting a nod from her as he turned toward the front door.

"Well, I don't really need it right *now*," Blaire called. But Aaron was already jogging down the front porch steps in the chilly air.

Holly slowly stood, holding Ivy close.

"I found this little baby blanket at the beach cottage; I hope you don't mind if we borrow it for a little while."

"Honey, I don't mind one bit. You can *keep* it, for that matter. Anything you need that I've got…well, it's yours!"

Blaire had a strong, bold voice. She gave Holly the impression that her confidence was something that had come with a full life, well-lived. She seemed to have joy that was nestled deep down. She had loved and had been loved fiercely, Holly thought.

Blaire reminded Holly of a hot cup full of apple cider that warms your gullet and satisfies all of your senses at once.

As they crossed the living room and neared the bottom of the staircase, Blaire stopped. "Now, I don't really want you climbing these stairs, but I guess there's not much choice. There are no bedrooms on the main level. But let's take it slow…and no more trips up and down than absolutely necessary, promise?" Blaire had started up the stairs slowly, with Holly following behind.

"I promise," Holly answered.

"Here, let me get behind you in case you were to fall. You can't hold onto the railing and hold the baby, too."

Blaire stayed one step behind Holly and Ivy until

they reached the second floor.

"All right," Blaire said as she stepped up even with Holly.

"This is my room," she said, pointing to the first room at the top of the stairs. The wide floor planks creaked as they walked across them.

"And this will be yours and little Ivy's room," she beamed, pointing to the bedroom right next to Blaire and Joseph's. Inside the room was a twin-sized bed, covered with a beautiful red chenille bedspread. The nightstand held a glowing, hobnail lamp that warmly illuminated the small bedroom. A cherrywood writing desk sat next to the window that faced the front of the house. At the foot of the bed was a cedar chest, just like the one at the beach cottage. Laying across it was a magenta pink and white checked flannel night gown and a pair of wool socks.

"These are for you," she said with a smile as she pointed to the clothing.

"Thank you!" Holly exclaimed. She couldn't wait to slip into the gown and lie in the bed beneath the inviting chenille bedspread.

"There are extra blankets and quilts in this chest, if you need them," said Blaire.

"And this...." Blaire said, walking around the chest to the other side of the bed.

"Is for the little one...I just happen to have a real strong desire for a grandbaby," Blaire admitted with a chuckle as she ran her hand along the beautiful polished wood of the baby cradle. Standing next to the bed, the cradle rocked, hanging in its stand. Inside it was a tiny mattress pad, covered with a maroon-colored sheet speckled with dozens of little white hearts.

"Oh, it's *beautiful!*" Holly said, following Blaire to the cradle. She ran her hand along the slick wood and gently swung it back and forth.

"*My* babies never slept anywhere other than in my bed with me until they were toddlers, but maybe little Ivy will," Blaire said, admiring Ivy in Holly's arms. "Anyway, it's here if you want to use it." She smiled a kind, warm smile. Holly was thankful to have found her in her time of much need. She couldn't imagine if the beach cottage had belonged to someone else, and she had been forced out with the baby. Or if Colt had found her. Her mind played out several different ways in which things could have gone differently, and each of them made her more thankful for the way things turned out.

"Your home is so beautiful and… happy," Holly said.

"I cannot thank you enough for allowing me to stay here."

"You're most welcome," Blaire said, placing a warm, soft hand over Holly's.

"And there's going to be no eviction notice," she added. "You and Ivy will have a home here as long as you need one."

Holly felt the sting of tears returning to her eyes.

She had a place to call home, once again. And Holly thought that it must be the best home in all the world.

ELEVEN

Christmas came and went, and it was the strangest, most wonderful Christmas Holly had ever had. Though she had precious memories from the richly abundant life she lived with Grandpa, Holly had felt something else this year that she had never felt before. Perhaps it was the fact that baby Ivy was with her, filling her heart with more love than she knew was possible.

Blaire had done something special every day leading up to Christmas, and she had included Holly in those things. One day, they strung dried orange slices into a garland, which they hung from all the curtain rods in the main living areas. The next day, they baked all day. There were peanut butter balls that they dipped into melted chocolate. There was toffee. There were Blaire's favorite gingersnap cookies, which reminded Holly of the ones she had made at the beach cottage and never even got to enjoy a single one of. She had told Blaire about making them after reading Aaron's birth story in the diary. Blaire wasn't upset with Holly for reading her diary, nor was she upset with her for hiding out in the beach cottage, or for using the groceries and the electricity in the house. When Holly apologized for each and suggested that Blaire may be offended, Blaire had laughed and hugged Holly tightly.

"You silly girl," Blaire said. "I am so glad you found your way to us." Holly felt at that moment as though her heart could burst right open.

The day after that, they stayed up until midnight, wrapping gifts that Blaire had brought out of her hiding place beneath the staircase. She carried out an armful of wrapping paper rolls, ribbons, and tape, and they both sat on the floor by the woodstove, wrapping the gifts while baby Ivy slept on the large tapestry ottoman nearby.

On Christmas Eve, Blaire had gotten up before daylight and started preparing the feast. Holly awoke to the smell of bacon and coffee floating upstairs and stirring her about. She nursed Ivy before getting dressed and heading slowly down the stairs, holding the baby in her soft blanket to her chest. Blaire greeted Holly with a plate full of bacon, eggs, toast, and a hot, steamy cup of coffee.

"Merry Christmas Eve!" she said excitedly. The lights were turned off, other than the kitchen light, which flooded into the adjacent living room. The wood stove in the corner flickered and crackled, warming the large farmhouse.

"I'm so excited. This is one of my favorite days of

the year," Blaire exclaimed.

Holly was filled with a new excitement as well. It was hard to resist the feelings of the Christmas spirit in Blaire's home. In addition to the mouthwatering smells and the warm, comforting fire, there was fresh garland hanging everywhere, candlesticks flickering about the house, and the low, merry sound of fiddles playing Christmas carols in the background.

Holly spent the day alongside Blaire as she prepared the ham, a multitude of sides, and the eggnog. Blaire relentlessly insisted that Holly stay seated on the couch by the fire.

"You just go lie back and hold that sweet baby of yours," she had said with a cheery smile. "I know you want to help, but it's important you do exactly as I tell you. What she had said next, though, is what made Holly's heart lunge.

"...You can help me next year. Though we'll have a toddler on our hands that we'll be trying to keep out of everything!" Blaire cackled, but Holly lay her head back on the cushion and smiled at the thought of staying there.

Aaron had spent most of his time outdoors, either by himself or alongside Joseph, but he came in to warm up and have meals with the women. Holly watched Aaron inconspicuously, mystified by the parts of him that she didn't know; fascinated by the parts she did.

He seemed to involuntarily mimic his father, making it seem as though he were years older than he actually was. He possessed wisdom beyond his youth, a stark contrast to any boy she had ever known. His calloused hands told the story of hard, meaningful work, as he briskly rubbed them together in front of the black wood stove.

That evening, just as it was beginning to get dark out, Violet and her family arrived for the annual Christmas Eve supper. It was Violet and her burly husband, John, and all six of their adult children. Some of them brought spouses, and others were not yet married. Blaire's daughters and their husbands arrived shortly after, carrying armloads of gifts as they piled just inside the front door. Blaire's house was filled to the brim with family, Christmas cheer, and a love that radiated from wall to wall.

Everyone was eagerly curious about Holly, each making sure to take their turn speaking with her as she attempted to sink back into the shadows with baby Ivy. Violet was as warm and delightful as her sister, Blaire. She sat beside Holly and Ivy on the couch for quite a while, listening to Holly's side of the story that Blaire had already told her.

"I am just so glad you stumbled into our beach cottage," Violet said solemnly. She looked as though she might cry as she said it.

"Welcome to our family, Holly…and Ivy," she said, smiling as she stroked the baby's soft cheek. Holly then felt as though she might cry, too.

After the dinner, the house was full of laughter and

the clinking of dishes as Blaire and Violet began to clean up the remnants of the hearty dinner. Everyone present at the gathering was very conscious of Holly's need to be the one to hold her baby close, and sought the sure approval from Holly before touching baby Ivy. Holly appreciated that deeply, which only made her more comfortable letting Violet, Blaire, and Maeve each have a turn holding Ivy. She was happy to let them hold her as she sat close by, watching Ivy's perfect eyes look all around, blinking slowly and sleepily, happy and content as she ever was.

When Christmas morning came, Holly awoke right about daybreak. She sat up in the twin bed and stretched as she looked over in the dim glow the room held and checked on little Ivy. Sleeping peacefully in her little wooden cradle, her perfect little pink mouth suckled in her sleep. She gave the cradle a light push, letting it rock itself as she rose from the bed and walked to the frosty window that overlooked the spacious front yard. Holly pulled the curtains open, and to her utmost delight, saw large flakes of snow falling steadily. The brown grass was beginning to gain white patches as the snow accumulated on the ground. Holly's eyes lit up at the beautiful sight of a white Christmas morning.

The smell of fresh cinnamon rolls baking wafted up the stairs and filled Holly's bedroom as she picked baby Ivy up from her cradle and changed her tiny diaper. After nursing her, the two of them quietly headed downstairs to find Blaire, with Holly smiling all the way. She knew she would be sent to sit down before too long, but she didn't mind watching Blaire work in the kitchen from the cozy spot on the couch. She dreamed of the day when she would be alongside Blaire, helping to prepare meals together. Although she just wasn't completely sure if that would ever come to be, it was most thrilling to hope for.

"Good morning!" Holly sang as she entered the toasty-warm living room next to the kitchen where Blaire was working. The kitchen gave a shadowy light to the dark room.

"*Good morning!* And Merry Christmas!" Blaire exclaimed with a wide, warm smile. She kneaded a ball of bread on her countertop workspace, pausing to rub her forehead with the back of a floured hand.

"Did you and the baby sleep good?" she asked with genuine curiosity.

"Oh, yes. We slept *so* good," Holly answered.

"I know I never hear a peep out of that precious little girl at night." Blaire nodded toward Ivy, bunched up in Holly's arms.

"I guess she has everything she needs," Holly said with a shrug. "I nurse her pretty often, but she's right there in bed with me for most of the night, so it's really no trouble."

"That's exactly right... Good girl. That is one lucky little baby." Blaire winked at Holly as she continued kneading the dough.

The faint, soft sound of banjos and fiddles played

Christmas songs from Blaire's kitchen radio as Blaire danced around from task to task. Holly watched and chatted, knowing better than to ask if she could help. Blaire was very serious about Holly's resting period.

Soon, the men of the house thundered in the front door, startling Ivy for a moment and bringing a cold gust of wind with them. The snow was still coming down like someone was in the sky plucking a goose. The snowflakes on the mens' boots and coat sleeves immediately began to melt as they stepped into the warmth of the house.

"Ooh, shut that door!" Blaire scolded playfully.

Aaron carried a large, silver bucket full of fresh milk across the living room into the kitchen, where he set it on the counter by the sink.

"Thank you, son," Blaire said as she worked the dough.

Joseph and Aaron both stood in front of the stove with four large hands outstretched toward the radiant warmth of it.

"Are the cows happy?" Blaire asked.

"Happy as can be," Joseph answered. "They've got plenty of hay in the barn and the electric warmer in their water trough."

"Good. I want them to be all cozy. I still can't believe we're getting a white Christmas!" Blaire shrieked with delight as she tapped her feet on the floor.

Aaron turned to face Holly before slowly walking over and taking a seat next to her. He leaned forward as he sat, with his forearms propped on his knees. He spoke to Holly without looking at her.

"Well, here's your white Christmas," he said with a half-smile.

"I can hardly believe it," Holly replied. "It's just like home. Only somehow, it's even better."

Holly didn't believe Grandpa would be offended if he could have heard her say that. He knew that while he was giving her the best upbringing that he possibly could, she would someday fly the coop, and he had hoped that she would be setting out for something even grander than the satisfying days of her youth.

The last several months had been questionable for her. The last several days, even more so. Holly wasn't sure at times where she would lay her head down at night, or where her next meal would come from. But Blaire promised her that neither of those things would ever be of concern to her again, as long as she had anything to do with it. That was part of the reason this was Holly's best Christmas yet. The other part of the reason was lying peacefully in her arms, looking up at her with blue eyes as she held her tiny hands next to her face.

Aaron didn't say anything else. Instead, he leaned over and gently caressed baby Ivy's arm for the first time. He hadn't had much interest in holding her or even outwardly admiring her before. Holly stole a glance at Blaire, who gave her another wink.

"Do you want to hold her?" Holly asked Aaron.

"I, uh…Well, sure," he replied with a half shrug.

As Holly gently passed the baby to him, he awkwardly arranged his hands a couple of times before deciding on a proper grasp of the tiny baby.

"Aaron, I declare!" Blaire said as she tossed a hand towel over her shoulder and stepped into the living room. She stood with her hands on her hips.

"I do believe little Ivy here is the first baby you have ever held, isn't she?"

Blaire turned to Holly. "He's always been scared to death of babies."

Holly snickered. "You know, I believe it. The way he pored over that car seat manual. I'm surprised he let us ride with him to buy it."

"Real funny," Aaron responded. "I don't know why, but I just felt like I needed to take ya'll and get out of there for some reason. I wasn't all that worried about the car seat at the time."

At the sound of the kitchen timer, Blaire spun around and headed straight for the oven. She pulled out a pan of fresh, homemade cinnamon rolls that smelled absolutely divine. She took a small pitcher from the countertop and drizzled the warm, white frosting over the hot dessert.

"Oh, this is going to be *so* good. I can almost taste it now," Blaire said.

"It sure smells good," Joseph said as he turned to face her, his back to the hot stove.

Blaire looked over at Holly. "This is a family

tradition," she explained. "I make cinnamon rolls every Christmas morning. It used to be all of us, of course. But the girls all wanted to start their own 'Christmas morning traditions,' so now we have everyone over for Christmas Eve, and I spend Christmas Day with my boys."

"And now… you and sweet Ivy," she added with a grin.

After the four of them devoured the square pan full of hot cinnamon rolls with farm-fresh milk, Blaire announced that it was time to open gifts. First, she reached underneath the illuminated tree for a small gift wrapped in green paper with a red ribbon tied around it. She handed it to Holly. "I wish I had known you would be here with us sooner, because then I would have had time to go out and buy a better gift for you," she said.

"But this is something I think you'll like."

Holly looked ashamed. "You shouldn't have, Blaire. I have all I need in the world because of you and your family."

"Sweet girl." Blaire patted Holly's knee. "It's not much, but a young lady like you needs one of those. Trust me… you're a lot like me."

Holly turned to Aaron, who was sitting next to her again, and offered him baby Ivy. He gently took her, a little more comfortable the second time.

Then she carefully opened the gift to find a beautiful leather-bound book with carvings of wheat stalks on the front of it. Quickly flipping through it, she found that the book was full of blank pages for her to fill.

"It's your very own diary," Blaire explained.

"I hope you like it."

"Oh, thank you! I love it. I haven't journaled in so very long, and I have quite a bit of catching up to do," Holly said, admiring baby Ivy, who was lying peacefully on Aaron's muscular forearms.

"You're very welcome," Blaire replied with a warm smile.

As the family exchanged gifts, Holly sat back on the large, comfortable sofa and smiled as she was filled with peace and joy. Though she was not quite sure what the future would hold, and how long she would be with Blaire and her family, she was living for the here and now, and it was wonderful.

TWELVE

The sound of the telephone ringing startled everyone in the room. It was the first time since Holly had been with the family at the farmhouse that she had seen or heard a phone at all. Blaire quickly stood from the rocking chair and went to the rolltop desk in the corner of the living room, where she retrieved her ringing phone.

"That's Horace," Blaire said to Joseph with a puzzled look on her face.

Joseph reflected her confused expression as the family listened to Blaire's end of the conversation.

"Hello?"

"Merry Christmas to *you*, Horace. How are you and Jan?"

"Huh? Well, what is it? What's the matter?"

"Oh, my goodness…Oh, no... Are you and Jan all right?"

Blaire held her palm to her forehead as she looked at Joseph.

"Okay. We'll be on the way just as soon as we can.

Yes. We'll be there in a couple of hours."

"Bye-bye."

Blaire ended the call and stuffed the phone into the pocket of her sweater.

"What *is it?*" Joseph asked, moving toward her.

"Horace said the beach cottage was ransacked, and then the burglar was hit by a car and killed, right in front of the house!"

"We've got to get down there. He said the police may be calling me, but they would really like for me to go down and speak with them…take a look at the damage and file a report. They couldn't get a hold of Violet – I am sure she has her phone turned off. The kids are all gathered at her house."

"What in the world?" Joseph said, shaking his head.

Blaire turned to Holly.

"Holly…Would you rather go with us or stay? I don't want you to make the trip, especially in this weather. But I don't want to leave you and the baby here alone, either."

"I'll stay with them," Aaron quickly offered.

"If that's okay with you," he added, looking at Holly.

"That's fine by me." Holly looked at Blaire and nodded. "But I'll do whatever you think is best."

"I think that's a wonderful idea, Aaron. You and Ivy will be in good hands with Aaron while Joseph and I are gone."

Blaire untied her apron and tossed it onto the kitchen counter as she continued. "We will be back just as soon as we can. Holly, if you get hungry, let Aaron know. He will be glad to fix you something."

Taking a set of keys from the hook by the door, with her purse on her shoulder, she stood on the rug, waiting for Joseph.

"Come on," she said, motioning for him.

"I'm coming. Can't I make a cup of coffee to go? It's not *that* urgent is it?"

Blaire rolled her eyes, but she wore a smile.

"Oh, I'll make it. Put your boots on."

Blaire tossed the keys into her purse and set it on the floor before heading back into the kitchen.

"Luckily, the ole *BUNN* works fast. I'm making a whole pot, so ya'll have the rest," she called to Holly and Aaron.

Soon, Blaire and Joseph were off into the white wonderland that lay quietly outside the door. The snow continued to fall and drift in the light wind.

Holly turned to Aaron. "Well, that's pretty disturbing, considering I was just in that house a short few days ago…what if it had happened while Ivy and I were in there?" Her eyes grew wide.

"Well, let's just be thankful that it *didn't* happen while the two of you were in there. Although I'm sure you were a little bit scared when I came walking in. You didn't know me from Adam's house cat."

Holly snickered. "It's a funny thing, you know. I

wasn't scared. I heard you unlock the front door and come in. Heard you walk slowly across the kitchen floor, getting closer. I knew someone would eventually come, but I didn't think it would be so soon. And I definitely didn't think it would be *you*."

"Are you glad it was?" Aaron asked shyly as he stared down at Ivy.

"Am I *glad*?" Holly scoffed.

"I'm more than glad, I can promise you that," she assured him.

"I mean…" he fidgeted. "Wouldn't you rather it had been Mama–or…or Aunt Violet who had come for you?"

Holly was quiet for a moment, only to make him wonder.

"Noooo, I don't wish it had been your mama or your aunt Violet," Holly said with a smile, as she playfully pushed his shoulder.

At this, Aaron blushed as a broad grin spread across his face.

"I wouldn't be here with you now if I didn't trust you."

The grin slowly melted into a bit of a somber expression before he quickly spoke again, his tone suddenly lively.

"I have to admit it; it scared me just a little bit when I realized somebody was in the house. I sure didn't expect there to be." He snickered.

"You? Scared?"

"Yeah, I was – spooked, okay? Spooked would be a better word, I guess."

Holly laughed and repositioned herself where she sat in the corner of the L-shaped couch.

Aaron continued to hold sleeping baby Ivy as he and Holly talked in depth about their own separate lives. Though Holly had known a good bit about the heart of Aaron just from reading about him in his mother's diary, she was beginning to see and to know an intimate side of him. Intimate, yet innocent.

Holly wondered if she could call herself innocent after what had happened with Colt. She hadn't asked for it, but he didn't ask either. He just took, leaving her feeling disgusting and hurt. One thing he gave her, without meaning to, was her baby girl.

Beneath all the love and joy and peace that Holly felt as of late, fear was buried deep underneath it all, waiting to rear its ugly head. She wondered if she would ever completely stop being afraid that he would find them. She wasn't afraid for herself; she was beginning to feel that Aaron would keep her safe. Blaire and Joseph would, as well. There was no question about that. What she feared was that he would learn that she had a baby, and demand testing to determine if he was the father. Holly shuddered at the thought.

The sound of the home telephone ringing broke into Holly's thoughts, startling her. Aaron carefully but quickly passed baby Ivy to Holly before taking long strides across the living room and retrieving the telephone from the kitchen.

"It's Mama," he said, before bringing the phone to his ear.

"Is it bad?" he asked Blaire, on the other end.

They had left more than three hours ago.

"Mmhmm."

"Gracious, that's just awful."

"All right. I'll turn it on right now."

"They're good."

He smiled at Holly.

"We're all good. I'll warm us some supper. Don't worry."

"Did you ever get a hold of Aunt Violet?"

"Mmhmm. Good."

"Okay. I love you. Bye."

Aaron pressed the button to end the call before walking back into the living room.

"Mama said for us to turn on the news," he said, looking around in search of the TV remote. "They're about to do an interview, and it's going to be a live broadcast."

"My *goodness*," Holly said. "What else did she say? How does it look down there?"

"She said nothing was stolen that they could tell; he just busted the lock and shuffled things around in the house, pulled everything out of the closet, and knocked over a lamp or something."

"That is so bizarre. I wonder if he was drunk or something," Holly said, bewildered.

Aaron clicked on the television and scanned the stations before landing on one. Just as he did, both of them recognized the street view on the television. The female news reporter's voice came across loudly.

"We have a breaking news story this afternoon out of Hope County – a tragedy on this Christmas Day. We're LIVE from Saltwater Street, here at the scene of a fatal accident following multiple home invasions right here on this very street."

The camera panned to the familiar yellow beach cottage as the news reporter began questioning an elderly man in a red sweater-vest.

"That's Horace. He lives right next door to the beach cottage," Aaron said, keeping his eyes on the television.

"What can you tell me about the incident that occurred this morning?"

The reporter pushed a microphone into Horace's face.

"My family and I were just gathered in the kitchen when we heard a loud calamity coming from the front door. I went to check, and it was the young man who has since been in a terrible accident. He looked wild-eyed, he smelled like alcohol, and his hair looked like it hadn't been brushed in weeks. When he saw me going toward him, he commenced yelling nonsense, looking around, and flailing. He kept looking for someone named Holly. 'Holly! Holly! Are you in here?' he kept yelling, over and over. I told him to get out of my house, and that's when he started trying to fight me. He didn't have the strength, though. He stumbled back out the door, still swinging at the air, and shuffled out into the street, where he was struck by that minivan. That's all I know…It's a really unfortunate situation. I will never get that picture out of my head. I called the ambulance right away, but he was dead at the scene, they said."

The camera flashed back to the reporter.

"Officials are telling me that the victim has now been identified as twenty-five-year-old

Colt Williams of Sevier County, Tennessee….

Holly didn't hear anything else that was said. She could feel the blood draining from her face as her heart pounded within her chest. She stared, wide-eyed at the television, a knot forming in her throat.

"Are you okay?" Aaron asked.

"Holly? Are you okay?"

Holly slowly looked over at him in disbelief.

"That's him," she whispered. "Colt came after me. He had tracked me down…" Holly began to tremble as tears poured from her eyes and down her cheeks. Aaron placed his large, warm hand on her back as she struggled to catch her breath.

"He–he–he…." Holly couldn't get the words to come out.

"But you came for me. You rescued me," she blubbered.

Aaron was silent as Holly crumbled against his

chest, where she wept for several long minutes. Baby Ivy slept soundly on the couch next to Holly, never sensing the disturbance.

"Shhh," Aaron attempted to soothe her as she squalled into his t-shirt.

Between the sound of his heartbeat and his gentle shushes, Holly was finally able to gain her composure. Sitting upright, she wiped both cheeks, but tears continued to cloud her eyes.

"We were just there…I just knew we were safe there. He would have killed me if you hadn't come, and who knows what would have happened to her…" Holly's words were choked off again as she looked down at Ivy. But she didn't need to say anything more; Aaron knew how she must be feeling.

He was in disbelief himself, and it was making chilling sense now why he felt so rushed to get Holly and baby Ivy out of the cottage. Colt would have broken into the house just three or four days after he'd brought them home with him.

"How did he ever track us down? I don't believe it; I didn't leave a trace…"

Aaron spoke for the first time. "It doesn't matter now…It's all going to be okay, now."

He wrapped his strong, muscular arm around her shaky shoulders. With sleeping baby Ivy lying next to her, Holly folded into Aaron, where she felt completely safe, and wept until she fell fast asleep.

THIRTEEN

Dear Diary,

It's me...Holly. I haven't written in a diary for so long, but I think it's time. My life has taken so many unexpected turns as of late, but they have collectively led me here...and here is nothing short of superb.

Ten months have elapsed since I moved in with the Bakers...Aaron, Blaire, and Joseph. I simply cannot imagine being anywhere else, and I count myself extremely fortunate to have been given the gift of raising my daughter here in the happiest place in the whole world.

I remember, with sympathy, the days when I wandered the streets alone, pregnant, essentially homeless, and looking over my shoulder with every step, fearful that somehow my abuser would be there, stalking in the darkness...waiting to attack.

But in the unlikeliest and most fortunate of circumstances, I happened upon the unlocked beach cottage that became my shelter and my birth place. I was and continue to be tremendously grateful for the presence of the beach cottage. I found solace within the walls of the home, as it provided nourishment, warmth, and shelter in my time of great need for all of the above.

When Aaron came in and found me there, just hours after I had given birth to Ivy, I felt indebted to him and to his family. They were so wonderful and merciful to welcome me into their tranquil home with utmost hospitality. The extreme peace that blanketed me as I became a member of this household was something I had never quite felt before. Perhaps it was the stark contrast of my previous living situation to the one I was stepping into that made it so much sweeter.

In addition to my savior, Aaron, coming to my aid in my great time of need, I received the greatest Christmas gift one could ever possibly dream of...my Ivy. Born just a few days before Christmas, she has been my absolute joy and focus. Caring for her is my most important duty, and one that I take oh-so seriously. At times, I find it difficult to believe that I actually get to shape the life of the most beautiful girl in the world.

Blaire has been more helpful to me than I can put into writing. She has become like the mother I never had. She has said herself, more than once, that she and I share so many personality traits because we were both raised without a mother. We agree that it has made for two strong-willed women, both feeling a little bit like there's always been a missing piece, and yearning to stitch that missing piece into our own families.

I have been lucky enough to receive the gift of motherhood myself, but also the gift of Blaire and her wise, wonderful mentorship. There has not been a single thing that has come up in our many conversations that she hasn't had an experienced opinion about. And though I have not known her for very long, I trust her. I have trusted Blaire, Aaron, and Joseph ever since the first day I met them. I know that seems unlikely for such a girl as myself...with such a traumatic past history as I have, but somehow everything has felt so easy with them, even from the very beginning.

Perhaps part of the reason the family earned my immediate trust was that I had already taken a glimpse of Blaire's innermost thoughts as I read her diary that she had left behind at the beach cottage.

She wrote about Aaron, his kind heart, and his gentle way. I wasn't even frightened when he came for me. As I reflect on the exact moment and the moments leading up to Aaron entering the front door and walking in to find Ivy and me, it's chilling to realize that it could have very easily been Colt. I had no fear or thought of it being him when I had heard the front door creak open, but in hindsight, I should have. Had Aaron not come and rescued us, Colt would have been the one to enter the house and find us there, so delicate and vulnerable. I shudder at the thought of that.

Over the course of the last ten months that I have been living here in North Carolina, I have learned some interesting bits of information, beginning with the big question of how Colt ever hunted me down in the first place. Although it's not necessarily important anymore, my curiosity was satisfied when I spoke with some authorities from Tennessee who had come in search of me.

Apparently, without my knowing —or caring—a lawyer from back in Tennessee had been trying to locate me regarding Grandpa's estate. During their search for me, they somehow gathered that Colt and I had been associated with one another at one time, and so they went knocking on his door. Together, they managed to obtain enough information from unknowing employees at the bus station, who had said that someone matching my description was seen buying a ticket and boarding a bus bound for Hope County, South Carolina.

Colt then broke into Grandpa's old house and stole one of my old T-shirts, borrowed his buddy's hound dog, which he passed off as a service dog on the bus ride, and quite literally had me sniffed out. In order to successfully pull it off, it must have been one of those rare occasions in which Colt was halfway sober.

Later, after the chaos of the break-in and accident had simmered down, someone found the hound dog aimlessly wandering around in one of the neighbors' yards. They managed to return him to his rightful owner.

Now that I have recorded the unbelievable events that have impacted my life lately regarding Colt Williams, I declare here and now that I will not ever speak of or write of him again.

Regarding the events that have impacted my life lately, there is something else that has recently taken place, and it is far more pleasant than the last. It is the real reason for my desire to begin journaling tonight. I could just hardly wait to sit alone with my thoughts and attempt to write down what I'm feeling, because I don't ever want to forget this day.

It began as most mornings do these days. Ivy and I awoke right about the break of day. After diapering and nursing the baby, I got myself dressed for the day, brushed my hair, and then the two of us headed downstairs to find Blaire in the kitchen. While little Ivy played happily in her bouncy seat next to us, Blaire and I prepared the family's breakfast. While she scrambled eggs and toasted muffins, I started the coffee and set the table.

The morning sounds filled the house. Clinking dishes, sizzling butter, and a happy baby, contentedly playing with her own two chubby bare feet. It was a cloudy October day, the sun hiding behind thick blankets of gray clouds that seemed to hover above in layers. The darkened morning made for a pleasant moodiness that hung in the air like Christmas Eve.

Aaron and Joseph emerged at the same time, greeting us with hearty 'good mornings' and appetites alike. We sat down to breakfast as we usually do. The men had planned to work on fence repairs today, among other tasks they had discussed over breakfast while my mind was busy tending to Ivy's needs.

Just as Blaire and I were finishing up with the cleaning of the breakfast dishes and getting everything put back in order, Aaron cracked the front door. We both looked up at him, awaiting his request...

'Mama, could you get my denim shirt?'

*'Holly, would you mind bringing my **old** hat? I've got dirty boots on...'*

But it was neither of those things, nor any other favor. Instead, he simply said,

"Holly?"

Both Blaire and I looked expectantly at him, and then at one another.

I looked back at Aaron, waiting for him to continue.

"Uh. Um. C-could you come out to the b-barn for a minute?" he stammered.

"Are you alright?" I asked as I chortled. I looked at Blaire, expecting her to look as confused as I was. Her face didn't read confusion, but something more like amusement instead.

"Could you watch Ivy for a minute?" I asked Blaire with a shrug.

In response, Blaire beamed and held her hands out

for Ivy, winking at me as I passed the baby to her.

I went toward Aaron, who was waiting half inside and half outside the front door, just as he had been ever since resurfacing from his chores.

"I thought ya'll were working on stuff. What could you possibly need my help with?" I asked as I walked alongside him toward the big red barn.

"I'm gonna climb up in the hay loft, and I'm gonna need you to stand underneath and– just…I'll show you. Come on, it will only take a minute."

"Well, all right. But let's hurry up because your mama wants me to help her make a huge batch of beeswax candles once Ivy goes down for a nap."

The two of us marched through the big square opening in the front of the barn. I silently wondered what nonsense he had up his sleeve today. The two of us had become the best of friends since my coming to live here. We had spent many hours together. Not long after my postpartum recovery period had ended, he began referring to me as his right hand on the farm. We shared in the chores, making them faster and more enjoyable. Blaire and Joseph never said a word about me earning my keep here, but I very much enjoy helping with all of the chores around the farm, as well as with the household duties.

As I stood at the bottom of the ladder, waiting for Aaron to explain exactly what it was I was supposed to be doing, he yelled,

"Holly? Could you come up here for a minute,

please?"

I will admit that I rolled my eyes and sighed with annoyance in secret before I began climbing the rungs of the splintery ladder.

When I reached the top, Aaron was just sitting there on a square bale of hay. His elbows propped on his knees, he appeared to be deep in thought about something. He certainly didn't look like he was too busy with the task at hand...whatever that was supposed to be.

"What?" I asked, still standing on the ladder. "What do you need?"

Aaron looked as if I had startled him or interrupted his thoughts.

"Uh. Can you come here?" he asked, looking up at me only momentarily and then back to his boots on the hay-covered floor.

Growing a bit more exasperated by his odd behavior and lack of any sort of explanation, I stomped over to him.

"Yes?" I crossed my arms. I hadn't exactly dressed for spending the rest of the day outdoors. 'Had I known how long this would take...' I thought.

"Holly...I want to ask you something. Now, you don't have to give me an answer right this minute or anything. I mean, you can think about it and whatnot. You can—"

My eyes widened as I awaited the question. I think I might have tapped my foot impatiently.

Just then, Aaron quickly stood. Facing me, he grasped both of my arms gently, and a bit shakily, I noticed.

"Would you—"

"Would you...marry me?"

I don't even think I have the proper words to write down to describe the way I felt at that very moment, but it was somewhere between astounded and jubilant. I am sure I looked at him with an awestruck expression, but he just stood very still, his shoulders tense as he held his breath and waited.

I gladly accepted his proposal, of course. I did not need to mull over his question, though it did take me quite by surprise. Aaron and I had shared many deep conversations, and I had always felt a strong bond with him. I liked everything about him, and deep down I had even felt a twinge of jealousy for whoever his future wife would come to be. I never considered the possibility that it could be me.

Aaron and I had never even shared a kiss until today...Though I think he almost kissed me once.

I had managed to fight back tears up until Aaron asked the next question, following the proposal. He asked me if he could adopt Ivy as his daughter.

How happy we will be to have such a strong and sensible man to take care of us. I can't wait to take care of him, too, just the way Blaire always has...for Aaron, and for Joseph.

Blaire was euphoric as she held Ivy and bounced

up and down on her heels the minute Aaron and I walked into the house wearing smiles from ear to ear. She had known his plans, of course.

Presently, we are all still floating high on clouds of exhilaration. We haven't talked about any plans just yet, but instead are looking forward to the decisions and tasks that lie shortly ahead. I suspect Aaron will want to build a house close by his parents, and that will be more than okay with me.

I cannot wait for our wedding day. I can't wait for Ivy to say his name: 'Daddy'.

I can't wait for her to have the things in life that I didn't have. I can't wait to have more of Aaron's children.

I just... can't wait.

Epilogue

Winter and Spring had come and gone. A June wedding in the Bakers' spacious country yard took place for the marriage of Aaron and Holly. A blonde-haired little Ivy toddled ahead of Holly, tossing daisy and zinnia petals from Blaire's garden. The ceremony was nothing short of beautiful and blissful. It was a small wedding, with only family and friends from Aaron's side present. Holly didn't invite any of her old friends from back home; she had said she was starting fresh with no connections to her past life, though she vowed to herself to carry the good memories with her always. She kept a secret hope that maybe she would make a couple of good friends in her new home, but realized completely that Blaire, Violet, and their daughters would offer all the warm friendship she could possibly ever need.

Since the wedding, Holly and Aaron had drawn up their own custom blueprint for the house they will build on the property Joseph and Blaire deeded to them as their wedding gift. It sits behind the Baker farm a good distance for walking, but with plenty of space for their own barn, pasture, and gardens.

Holly's nights are spent with Aaron, poring over the plans again and again, dreaming and doodling from their upstairs bedroom at the Bakers' home.

Little Ivy lights up everyone's life. She is especially fond of her Mimi Blaire, who wears Ivy wrapped tightly around her little finger everywhere she goes.

The time in which Blaire would be able to bring grandchildren to the beach came sooner than she had ever dreamed it would, and it was also even more special to her than she had imagined.

They ran along the sandy shore gathering shells and splashing in the salty water just this morning. Blaire and Holly had tried browsing the antique store in the afternoon, but were both a bit distracted by Ivy's babblings and mischievous handling of the many fragile items housed inside the tight quarters of the store…just as Blaire had known they would be.

Mimi Blaire didn't long for an uninterrupted shopping trip; she had gotten enough of those in between Aaron's childhood days and the present, and she knew she would probably see more quiet, long, lonesome days sometime in the future…she certainly wouldn't rush for them though.

Shortly after Aaron had proposed to Holly, the lawyer who had been in contact with Colt prior to his death finally located and spoke with Holly regarding her late Grandpa's estate. He had left everything he had owned to her, and he hadn't owed a single person for anything.

It was a sad decision for Holly to make, but she knew what had to be done, and she had been most grateful for the choices she had been given.

Holly sold the land, the house, the cattle stock, and most everything inside the house. She kept Grandpa's truck for Aaron and herself, remembering Grandpa fondly each time she climbs into the old Ford.

Aaron left his landscaping job and began driving a logging truck for a more suitable income for raising a family. With the money they had from selling Grandpa's estate, they could build their new home, and Aaron could have afforded to take some time off, but he refused. One of the many things Holly loves about her husband is his devotion to her and to Ivy.

As night fell on the quaint little beach cottage, the drapes in the bedroom swayed lightly in the breeze. Holly stood in front of the open window, allowing the breeze to comb through her salty hair as she held Ivy in her arms. She kissed the top of her blonde curls as she danced slowly back and forth, remembering the night Ivy was born in the very same room where she stood.

Holly carefully laid sleeping Ivy on the bed where she had taken her very first breath, and slowly tiptoed out of the room to join her family in the living room. As she sat in the circle of loved ones, Holly was blanketed with assurance and gratitude.

She knew that no matter what the past held, it couldn't touch her. Though the cottage might have looked just as it did the last time she was there, everything had changed.

From the author

In the story of The Primrose of Bascomb (Book 1), we are reminded of the comfort God provides to us when we seek after Him. Addie's words reached Blaire in her time of great need and offered comfort, which ultimately led to a deep joy that she had never felt before. God's Word also offers us comfort, and from that comes joy, and so much more.

When Blaire meets Violet in the story of Violet's Roots (Book 2), she is given steady direction as a new wife trying to gain her footing. We can compare this to the way in which we are called to lead and direct those newer in their faith than we are. Sometimes, we may forget or overlook just how important it is for us to lead others in discipleship. After all, we are commanded (not suggested) to do so!

Finally, The Deliverance of Holly aims to paint the picture of a full-circle achievement. Blaire's life had been changed through someone's words written in a lost diary, and in turn, she essentially changed someone else's life with her own written words. After many years, Blaire had finally become confident and wise in the things that she once viewed as daunting, and she was able to comfort a helpless Holly in her time of need.

*The gift we give when we pass on what we've been given reminds me of The Great Commission: Jesus' instructions to His disciples to **go** and to **teach.** Though the story of Holly and Blaire isn't one of teaching the gospel, we can use their example and pass along what we know to be true. Again, we aren't recommended to this; we're called to do this!*

Moreover, as you have read, Holly receives the greatest gift she has ever received just in time for Christmas —her baby, Ivy. Holly even receives an additional gift (Aaron) whom she calls her savior.

I love to think of my own Savior and how he rescued me personally from a life of destruction apart from Him. It is crucial to recognize our desperate <u>need</u> for a savior, and the only One just happens to be the greatest gift <u>we've</u> ever received...

Jesus Christ, who came as a newborn baby, born of a virgin in the city of Bethlehem, more than two thousand years ago...And He wants to be your Savior, too!

Author Bio: Taylor is a southern wife and mother who writes from her comforting home in South Carolina. Once a nurse, she now enjoys writing, gardening, cooking from scratch, and cultivating a beautiful life for her family. You can usually find Taylor with a baby in her arms or running around her feet as she tends the home and writes the story of their lives together.